To Richard and Sue

with every good wish

George

Metamorphosis of a Courtesan

GEORGES WASER

XANADU FICTION

© Georges Waser 2006
Metamorphosis of a Courtesan

ISBN   0-9553485-0-1
       978-0-9553485-0-1

Published by Xanadu Fiction
1 Roehampton Close
London
SW15 5LU

The right of Georges Waser to be identified as the author of this work has been asserted by him in accordance with the Copyright, Designs and Patents Act 1988.

All rights reserved. No part of this publication may be produced in any form or by any means – graphic, electronic or mechanical including photocopying, recording, taping or information storage and retrieval systems – without the prior permission, in writing, of the publisher.

A CIP catalogue record of this book can be obtained from the British Library.

Designed and produced by:
The Better Book Company Ltd
Forum House
Stirling Road
Chichester
West Sussex
PO19 7DN

Printed in England.

Contents

		Page
1.	The Lure of Things Past	1
2.	Prelude: At the Fountain of Light	2
3.	An Erroneous Judgement?	17
4.	Interlude: Three Graces and a Dark Lady	20
5.	Last Stop Down Memory Lane	52
6.	Fluentia Re-visited	55
7.	Of Paintings and Recipes	106
8.	The Temperature Rises	120
9.	Alpiniano's Cave	170
10.	A Nymph Turns Into Water	183

Ut pictura poesis.

Horace

1

The Lure of Things Past

When had he last read these notes? Maybe about seventeen years ago – which was more or less when he had written them down. Although he had never forgotten about them, it now came as a surprise to him that he did not really remember their contents. And certainly not the flowery style! Despite being moved, as he always was when faced with the past, Merten could not help pondering over his own outpour with slight amusement. Was it his youthful perception which had made him write like this? Or was it the place, utterly captivating as it had been on the occasion of his first visit? Anyway, he would soon know.

For the first time in many years, he was to go back for a couple of months rather than just a few days – not to Fluentia, but to a small place which, like Fonteluce, was situated in the hills surrounding the city. He knew that there he would regain his strength. The doctors told him that, at just about forty, he was likely to recover well; faster, anyhow, than most people who needed the kind of surgery he had undergone. Merten, sitting on the terrace of his ancestral home near Charlottenfels, gave in to temptation: he had to read his first ever attempt at writing a diary again. So far on this day, he had only leafed through the pages before him at random.

2

Prelude: At the Fountain of Light

Fonteluce, Saturday 24 March 19..

In the village they tell me that this place was built by Atlas, son of the Titan Iapetos. Built, my informants hasten to add, under a particularly favourable star: whoever comes here, they say, is supposed to find peace of mind, health and happiness.

Anyway, Fonteluce is full of atmosphere. In a gorge nearby my ancestors the Goths – some 200,000 men, on their way to the Eternal City – were utterly routed by Fluentia's sons. They surely did not find happiness! But there is also that other spot, near the foot of the hill, where two little streams meet; if a long dead poet is to be believed, these streamlets originated in a pair of metamorphosed lovers. Thus legend flows into history and history flows into legend – in Fonteluce, however, legend seems to predominate.

The villagers also say that once upon a time the surrounding forests were the haunts of the most excellent doctors of witchcraft. At a well – then frequented by the villagers' wives with their washing – these practitioners used to meet and graduate: strange creatures which carried with them eyes and heads exchangeable, very much the way people nowadays carry on them two or three different pairs of spectacles; creatures who, having converted into animals under a certain nut tree, were able to rise into the air. Sometimes, so I am told, these shapes of the night were even seen in downtown Fluentia, hovering above the dome of that city's great cathedral.

Moreover, there was this poet who lived at the foot of the hill of Fonteluce – not the one I have already referred to, but another who wrote that our souls are those angels who had remained neutral during Satan's revolt: angels consigned to our bodies by the Maker, so that they would ultimately have to choose between good and bad. Whether or not it inspires peace, the air of Fonteluce and its hillside seems most conducive to the mind!

Needless to say that today I feel special. I am writing on my birthday – which, according to the old calendar, was once upon a time the last day of the year in Fluentia. And to Fluentia I now want to turn. In fact, this truly magnificent city is said to owe its origins to Fonteluce: to some merchants who, for the sake of convenience, had left their dwellings on the hill and settled around what had started as a mere market-place in the plain. Small wonder Fluentia's history was later to become the history of a powerful house of merchants! As to thanks: eventually, just as my ancestors the Goths, Fonteluce too had to yield to Fluentia.

Although I arrived here but some three weeks ago, I already have a local: whenever I am in Fluentia, I spend some time drinking in the same little place, near the ancient temple of St. John the Baptist. I do not even know its name, but I remember that the sign – it was taken down last week, whatever the reason – showed a red goblet on a white background. I also believe that in the square right outside, which looks more like a short street, at one time both wine and oil used to be sold. Anyway, it is this place more than any other which imbues me with the spirit of Fluentia. It is vibrant with talk; the people who come here, virtually all men, are small-time artisans, drivers, casual labourers and even peasants – people always ready to tell or listen to a story. In fact storytelling, so I am assured, has always been the great passion in Fluentia. It was in the city's squares where the masters of this craft performed their feats; and what inevitably began with an invocation of the Holy Trinity is said to sometimes have ended by the performer being offered money (for such was the power of his tale) by a member of the audience, *so that he would not let Hector, or Dido, die. But back to my local. As to what is told there, my still somewhat imperfect grasp of the language at times gives me quite a headache. But more than once the host has 'translated' for me. People easily tolerate a stranger's limitations here – just as in my mother's country, which accounts for my middle name, friends have always tolerated my sometimes peculiar use of their language.*

It is of course at my host's near St. John the Baptist where I learn a lot about the people of Fluentia. Without fail, the talk goes back some four or five centuries, to a time when this city had no rival elsewhere in the world – and without fail a story becomes quite a different story when it is being told a second time. Whether it is the tale of a headsman, who, having with the third stroke still failed to decapitate his victim, received a whipping by the chief-executioner (and who – as indeed I only learnt when listening to the same story again – was subsequently torn into pieces by an enraged crowd); or whether it is the tale of a foreigner who walked naked into a baker's oven, and who remained equally unscathed when afterwards he washed his hands in boiling oil ... One story I am yet to hear a second time concerns a statue of the Holy Virgin, placed outside some thermal spa: apparently, this statue was one day seen to close its eyes – as if it did not want to behold the obscenities people went there to indulge in! I must say that those who tell me all this are quite as colourful as the characters in their stories. So how does one define the model citizen of glorious Fluentia? I have asked quite a few of them, and surprisingly they all agree. Their choice, they claim, would be a man who had in fact been a weakly youth: an artist who was also an athlete – who as a swordsman was to have no equal; who, according to some, would with an arrow-shot perforate the strongest coat of arms; who, with his left foot resting against Fluentia's cathedral, would throw an apple much higher even than the colossal cupola – and who, according to others, would break in horses and in the very process perform, on the animals' backs, the most incredible rope-dancer's acts. A citizen indeed after my own heart; not least because I, too, was once a delicate child ...

Whatever I hear at my local has a ring of the fantastic, and sometimes – like in Fonteluce – it seems to me that paganism is just round the corner. According to some priests, even in Fluentia's most enlightened age the city's rising generation knew Jupiter, Saturn, Venus and Cybele better than the Father, the Son and the Holy Ghost. And what, if not a touch of the pagan, am I to detect in those who used to have their own images made: tiny waxworks which, as a token of their devotion, they then deposited in the Church of the Virgin Mary! Anyway, in Fluentia it was once the custom of almost every well-to-do family to keep an astrologer – often some poor devil employed, if of no other use, to entertain his master's kids with horoscopes. However, this city also boasted of a man believed to be a match even for Simon Magus: a magician whose every wish came true and who, in the company of a soldier of fortune, had embarked on a twenty-year voyage far beyond the Columns of Hercules ... a journey that had no parallel, and which he nevertheless is said to have completed at the very moment of departure. Small wonder the city's entire population trembled when this man announced that he had seen four thousand bloodthirsty hounds, followed by a host of starved horsemen with in their midst a giant so tall that his head was invisible, all of them moving from afar towards fair Fluentia. And small wonder my head sometimes swims after an hour's talk at my local. From there I frequently go, in order to sober up, to a coffee house near the old market – it too is situated just a stone's throw from the ancient temple of St. John the Baptist.

In fact this very temple is said to originally have served a pagan cult. The tale goes that a statue of Mars on horseback, which stood on one of the city's bridges, first adorned the temple. When the bridge collapsed, the statue disappeared together with it in the river – and the strange thing is that after the city's destruction by the barbarians, Fluentia could only be rebuilt when the statue was found again. Which does not really sound all that odd, considering that Fluentia had first been built under the sign of Aries, with Mars in the ascendant. I must remember to say more about the temple of St. John the Baptist – but there is still so much I have not even touched upon.

As to stories: there is one among the fellows drinking at my local who unmistakably speaks with some authority – this is obvious from the others' rather reverent attitude towards him. I have not yet, however, managed to get acquainted with the man; either I am already engaged in conversation when he enters, or then I simply cannot get through to his corner (the place, always crowded, is very narrow along the till). Only once I caught part of his discourse. It was about some knight who, upon riding into Fluentia, saw his baby son high up in a window. He shouted to the wet nurse to let go of the child, but the woman would not dare. 'Throw him down!' the father commanded – whereupon the terrified nurse closed her eyes and did as she was told. The knight caught the brat in his arm, particularly delighted with the fact that his offspring had not even screamed. It was this same child who was to become one of Fluentia's greatest princes ... which I only realized when one of the bystanders took up the theme and turned the clock some fifty years forward. When on his deathbed, so I learnt, the said prince was asked by his wife why he kept his eyes closed. 'To get accustomed to darkness,' was his answer.

Fluentia's princes would make an endless topic. Their realm, I am told, never knew any peasant revolts – and whenever the genius of democracy was too much at large in Fluentia, it was the policy of these princes to inebriate their subjects with *celebrations.* How closely the fate of Fluentia and her rulers was linked is illustrated in the sinister omens which accompanied the death of yet another of the city's luminaries: a lion in this prince's menagerie was devoured by its companions, the dome of the cathedral was struck by lightning, and a woman was pursued through the streets by a bull with blazing nostrils. It seems that for all this the prince, arguably the most accomplished man of his age, was somehow to blame himself, since upon falling ill he had liberated a spirit whom for years he had held prisoner in a ring on his finger. As a last remedy, his physician administered a drink containing finely-ground diamonds to the prince. But neither man was saved: the physician was later found dead at the bottom of a well, I believe near the temple of St. John the Baptist.

I find it quite difficult to say what I think mirrors best the former magnificence of Fluentia. There was, for instance, this craze for animals of fashion: dogs and geese enjoyed the freedom of the most elegant salons, the former – their collars adorned with jewels – being kept to look after the latter. Courtyards and gardens abounded with fallow-deer and chamois, and if the words of a then famous visitor can be trusted, there were also porcupines and ostriches. And then of course there were these other 'animals of fashion', the courtesans. 'Pieces of flesh with eyes', they were called by a thundering cleric and moralizer, but I beg to differ: for was it not the company of some of them that was most coveted by both Fluentia's nobility and her men of letters? How, otherwise, would one of them have dared to dedicate her poetry to the very grand duke? By whom she was subsequently exempted from wearing the yellow veil which the law imposed upon her profession as a trade-mark ... But I digress. As to the splendour of the courtesans – which must be indicative of the splendour of the times – I shall try to employ the art of Fluentia's master-storytellers: such was, according to one of the at the time most distinguished voices, the rich array of a certain courtesan's residence, that a foreign ambassador who one day visited these premises – and who was overcome simultaneously by both their grandeur and a sudden irritation in his throat – spat on the face of one of his servants, for fear of soiling the carpets.

It strikes me that I have not yet put Fluentia's artists in their true light – and if the greatness of a city is to be measured by the greatness of her artists, then Fluentia was once indeed truly great. For instance, there was a painter of whom it was thought that he must have visited a terrestrial paradise, with permission there to recruit his models. And there was another painter, whose gift was such that when he was one of a party accidentally captured by a pirate, his captor made him a friend and heaped riches upon him. And there was yet another who in a neighbouring country became the protégé of the king – and who returned to Fluentia for the love of a haberdasher's wife! So graceful were this painter's saints and madonnas that when destruction was afoot in Fluentia's churches, it was one of his works which made the vandals lose heart. Then there was this artist – foremost a poet and philosopher – who claimed to have turned Fluentia into a new Athens single-handedly: one day, while singing some rhyme in praise of a youth, this man was seized by a fever, became delirious ... and, aged forty, expired. Alas, for the transience of individual genius! And there was this other great thinker – to be cut off in his prime as well – who was born with a circular flame above his head; a flame that vanished almost immediately and was justly seen as symbolical both of the child's brilliant future and of the man's short life. Finally, there was this architect considered mad: mad, because he meditated upon the possibility of providing Fluentia's cathedral with a double-vaulted dome, so that people could ascend in the space left in between. The madman's work of course still stands – I have been up there, for the first time, this very day.

Looking back through these pages, I feel that for one who came here attracted by the notion of "villeggiatura" – or should I say idleness? – I have been a fairly diligent student. Mostly so in Fluentia, since in Fonteluce there is nothing which compares with my local. And as in the latter I have somehow, although passively, become part of the dramatis personae, my report is not ended by a long way. So what, or whom, shall I next talk about? The man in the street? Priests? Feasts and celebrations? Maybe Fluentia's women? Given my natural disposition, I could not possibly pretend to ignore the daughters of Eve ...

Fonteluce, Sunday 25 March 19..

I was born just before midnight – which is the reason for my writing this down in instalments. I felt like having a quiet little celebration late last night; a few drinks, while playing some music – that was it. Actually, the day of my birth had been a Sunday: a fact – it brings me right back to my topic – I would keep very quiet about, had I seen the light in ancient Fluentia. Here – since no salt was available on that day – Sunday's child had a reputation for being daft! And children other than bright, I understand, were rather the exception in this city.

As I have already implied, today would have been the beginning of the new year in Fluentia; in the olden days, that is. Needless to say that curiosity guided my steps: I paid an early visit to my local. And there I gathered quite a few pieces of useful information as to what I intended to commit to paper next. I had only just arrived when the chap in the felt hat – the one who speaks with obvious authority – entered; but as always, the throng was impossible, and before I could accost the man, he was back in his usual corner, out of my reach.

I may as well admit that I am no longer surprised at anything I hear in Fluentia. People live outdoors here, hence meet and chat continually – the street, I am told, has always been their parlour. There were even times when everybody gambled in the streets, in spite of the stern disapproval of both ecclesiastical and temporal powers. One could without much exaggeration say that the cradle of lottery stood here! Be this as it may, there is no doubt that the common man too had his share in immortalizing Fluentia; for wasn't it he – and not the scholars – who first embraced the city's greatest poet ever? Only long after his death, this divine bard was to be duly honoured in the temple of St. John the Baptist. It seems, therefore, appropriate to me that the man in the street did not take his hat off to anyone; only when meeting a knight, a physician or a canon would he acknowledge the other by inclining his head, perhaps by putting a finger or two to his cap. Which does of course not mean that Fluentia's townsfolk lacked a sense of humility or reverence. On the contrary – as, for instance, is shown by the fact that the common man had a lot of time for the veneration of martyrs. Whether it was the saint whose teeth were broken by the executioner, or the one who shouted from the stake that she would prove herself perfect like gold in the fire; or whether it was that other saint who, incarcerated in a tower with only two windows, forced the walls to break asunder and provide a third opening, such being her observance of the Holy Trinity: these martyrs were altogether much admired by the people of Fluentia.

Equally venerated, however, was an animal: the lion. For the lion was an emblem of Fluentia's independence. So what should I make of the experience of that noblewoman who, when pregnant, dreamed of giving birth – in one of the city's churches – to an oversize male lion? Well, the boy whom the said lady subsequently delivered was the first one in this house of merchant princes to later become Father of the Church. Needless to say the occasion prompted the most lavish celebrations – and celebrations are the topic I now want to turn to. In festive Fluentia too, the lions played a prominent part, although in competition with bears, leopards, boars, wolves and bulls – and what, in the grand duke's square, sometimes turned into a kind of hunt, was enthusiastically watched by tens of thousands. Such celebrations, it was held, were proof of Fluentia's magnificence and caused the world to hold its breath. However, the world was not slow to contribute: thus a foreign monarch, I today learnt at my local, brought with him to one of these feasts turned hunt a legless knight, capable of walking on his buttocks. And greatly did the people of Fluentia marvel when they witnessed the same knight jump off his buttocks straight onto his horse – and from the saddle back to the ground again.

No doubt the feast among all the feasts in Fluentia was the one in honour of St. John the Baptist. Each year on the day of the Baptist, one hundred of Fluentia's subjects, proud cities among them, were required to offer a tribute; a kind of flag it was, a prize anyhow, to be won in the races which were held that day. How religiously Fluentia observed this custom I again only learnt today: when at war with one of her greatest rivals, her knights on the day of St. John the Baptist held races beneath the walls of the very city under siege. Nothing would distract them that day – and whoever had personal reasons to celebrate, be it a wedding or something of similar import, made the occasion coincide with the feast of St. John. One belief in particular is worth noting: as a prayer in the vernacular of ancient Fluentia reveals, it was the Baptist who was credited with the power of providing maidens and widows with a husband. Hence the fair sex made the most of the feast – according to my sources, Fluentia's generally beautiful women looked absolutely irresistible on that day.

The male youth of course also played a part in the game. Their passion was for fine clothes – red coat, velvet cap with feather, perfumed gloves, rings so numerous as to make their fingers disappear – and this part of the game was called 'to smarten up *for the ladies.'* And what did the young women who encouraged such behaviour look like? As to ideals of female beauty, it was the poets who had laid down the guidelines. However, whilst they almost unanimously held that it was the blondes who among the belles of Fluentia deserved most praise, there was some disagreement with regard to details. One poet, for instance, demanded that rather than arched a lady's eyebrows should be straight, whereas another wanted them to be thick in the centre and noticeably thinner towards ears and nose. Not surprisingly it was the former, a master of the erotic tale, who had much to say about a woman's eyes: he wanted them almond-shaped, with a vivid, even slightly roguish expression. The latter writer however had an interesting point to make about the mouth – not more than six of the upper teeth, he said, were to be seen when the lips were closed. Eventually this man, once a Benedictine friar, was to far surpass all other theorists of beauty; it therefore seems adequate to let him have the last say as to the female physique. According to him, those considered the beauties of the day had to have a white, longish neck, long legs, small – but not skinny – feet, a full bosom with underneath no evidence of ribs, and firm, well-developed hands, with nails extending beyond the fingertips like blades of a little knife.

It seems the men of Fluentia did not much fear these fingernails – for how, otherwise, would they have competed so recklessly for the favours of the female? Fancy that two men fought a duel over another man's wife while the city was at war and the enemy right outside its gates! In fact, a truce had been agreed to – in other words: no cannon would be fired on either side while these two gallants settled their dispute in the lists. The loser was later to have the distinction of being briefly visited by his beloved (her husband had given his consent) ... and hereafter died of a broken heart rather than of his wounds. But, to return to the ladies: what did those do who felt that nature had not *granted them every privilege? There were many remedies for imperfections, be these flowers believed to cure a face that had become lopsided through the owner's sleeping habits, be these lotions to soften the skin of a lady's hands.*

Fluentia's women, so I am assured, shunned no sacrifice and were inimitable in the practice of self-discipline; often, the lavish application of paint to their faces would prohibit them, all day long, from showing even the faintest smile.

Today I again spent some time at the coffee house which I briefly mentioned in last night's notes. There, my sobriety restored, I asked myself how my head would have coped with the output of Fluentia's master-storytellers, had I lived in their time. I did not, however, gain any particular insights.

Anyway, back to my local I went, where I was soon to learn something not about women, but about this city's saintly men. Given, as I said before, that vanity was so much at large in ancient Fluentia, I would naturally have assumed that the clerics had a field day. As indeed they did! Foremost one Dominican friar, a man with whose views I have already taken the liberty to disagree. Yet, this friar's rhetorical powers were such that his sermons in Fluentia's cathedral used to draw crowds of, it was estimated, in between thirteen and fourteen thousand people. When he proclaimed that to prove the truth of his prophecies, he would walk into a fire, his disciples were as eager to follow him there as other men were to follow their brides into the matrimonial chamber. Alas, it turned out that the friar was less enthusiastic than his devotees – and when the day of the ordeal by fire came, it was to be his last. It may be worth noting that this man had donned the religious habit because of rejected love; and that it had been during a conversation of his with a woman – a nun, that is – when the sky opened in front of him, providing him thus with divine inspiration. Anyway, many of his views did live on; for, after him, there was another friar who spoke of wars so devastating that whole nations would be swept away by rivers of blood, of famines so terrible that parents would eat their children alive, and of plagues which would leave only every seventh woman with the hope of finding a husband. I am told it was the latter message which had the most powerful effect on Fluentia. Sadly, this second friar's life was to end prematurely, too; the vehemence with which he would preach to sinners being such that one day – on a 31st of December – he expired at the very end of a sermon. Thus neither of these two clerics was to see the day when the people of Fluentia, having for the third time driven their princes out of the city, elected Jesus Christ their king.

It was at the very moment this last piece of intelligence had been imparted upon the drinkers at my local, when some fellow shouted that the Virgin Mary too had been a candidate in the election – but that twenty-four votes had gone against her. Who on earth, I asked myself, had denied her the title of Queen of Fluentia? Who had dared to vote against the mater salvatoris? An odd thought crossed my mind: could it be that even in an age as great as the one I am talking about, there were those in Fluentia who believed that women ought to be kept at bay?

It was then, as I was still pondering the issue, that the host, who had watched me, gave the chap with the pointed felt hat a wink in my direction. Oh yes, I almost forgot to mention it: it was this indefatigable orator who had spoken about Fluentia's priests – and since the place had been unusually quiet when I re-entered it, I had for the first time managed to follow his entire discourse. And now his gaze was right upon me! It suddenly struck me that he seemed to control what I called the local's dramatis personae almost at will: nobody in the whole place spoke a word when he addressed me. Might he enquire, he asked most courteously, where I lived? At Fonteluce, I answered at once – and then wanted to add something about the country I am from.

But he nodded, thus stopping me short. Of course, Fonteluce, he said; adding benignly that no doubt I was of northern origin. I acknowledged his guess with a smile, and there was a pause. Had I heard, he then asked, of that northerner, a man who came from afar – no doubt from farther than I, he emphasized in his peculiar manner of a clairvoyant – and who at Fonteluce once occupied the bishop's chair? A saint, he added, who was compared to Joshua. Surely, he persisted, I must have heard of how this holy man struck a mountain barren because, when he was at prayer one day, it shielded the sun from him; of how, when a thief had despoiled his church at Fonteluce, he caused the sacrilegious creature's face to turn backwards, his tongue to stiffen, his eyes to close and his grasping hands to contract ... until the wretch repented and returned the stolen treasures; surely I must have heard of how this bishop, when an old man, was surprised by a storm while riding to the church – and of how the rain spared his aged frame? No? 'Well,' my informant added, 'now you have heard of him. And since I can see that you are much interested, I shall even tell you the story of how this saintly northerner arrived at Fonteluce.' It was at this very instant that I recognized the speaker for what he is: he is a master-storyteller! A member – maybe the last one in Fluentia – of what I had thought a long dead vocation.

As his tale was to be some kind of a compliment to me, the drinkers who obstructed my view of the master-storyteller had instinctively stepped aside – and only now I saw that in the corner where he always stands the floor is slightly elevated. Like in ancient Fluentia, where the practitioners of his art used to hold forth on a little platform. As if he had guessed my thought, the storyteller quickly bent backwards and produced a small musical instrument from amid what appeared to be his belongings. It was, as in the hands of many a Fluentia storyteller before him, a lute! No doubt my surprise, obvious as it must have been, amused him. Yet he kept a straight face, beginning to strum a few chords. But an odd thing suddenly happened. Two men entered and said something about people on Fluentia's bridges hearing bells in the water. There was quite a stir amongst the regulars, and like all the others I was rather badly pushed about. What made matters worse was that the great bell of the cathedral started ringing and – as the door to the place always stands open – drowned everybody's voice. Eager to converse with my new friend, I tried to get through to his corner. However, when things eventually quietened down again, the chance to talk to him had gone. His little platform was empty – unnoticed by me, and maybe attracted by the news of what people reportedly heard on the bridges, the storyteller had left.

Well, these are some of the impressions of a newcomer to Fluentia. And yet: when I was on my way back to Fonteluce this afternoon, I felt as if ages, and not something like three weeks, had passed since my arrival. It has been a beautiful spring day, with the hill looking truly spectacular. I suddenly remembered that near the place where I was born children used to, on this very day, carry straw puppets around: puppets richly adorned with women's jewellery. The omission of this custom was believed to bring bad luck. But I was soon to think of the storyteller again. I actually passed near the church of that holy northerner, which I think is now some kind of a university. And soon, from a bend farther up on the hill, I looked down to the valley underneath the church – the same valley from which the at one time bishop, and before him my less fortunate ancestors the Goths, had first beheld Fonteluce. I decided to propose the Goths as a topic to my new friend the storyteller, whenever I met him again.

3

An Erroneous Judgement?

Merten did not remember why, after just two days, he had stopped writing. Anyway, what he had just read was obviously the result of a sentimental urge, given that he had set pen to paper on a birthday of his. Even now, almost two decades later, he tended to celebrate birthdays in his way: as occasions for contemplation rather than with great fanfare – unless, of course, the birthday boy or girl was a dear friend.

Once more, his mind travelled back. Still sitting on the terrace of his ancestral home near the small town of Charlottenfels, with his chronicle still in his hands, Merten pondered over what followed his early 'grand tour', of which Fluentia had been the final destination.

He had started studying the history of art – not in Fluentia, but at the distinguished university of a neighbouring province. However, having won the most coveted prize after only two years, he had lost his motivation and become an early dropout. Eventually, this time on a northbound train and with only half of his prize money left, he had arrived back in Fluentia. He did not remember his arrival – nor much of the first few months during which he tried to set himself up as an art and antiques dealer. Anyway, his manners must have appealed to the affluent Fluentia crowd, as his efforts were soon to bear fruit. Merten, mindful of the flowery language in his diary pages, became pensive again: he knew that he had always had a showman's tendency. But he was not given to wildly theatrical displays. Not even when he was much younger – in spite of, he thought, this embroidered account before him. Suddenly, he was struck by an idea. Perhaps, when back in the hills near Fluentia in two weeks' time, he ought to start writing a diary again? It would be interesting to see to what extent his impressions – in other words: the then and now – differed.

He put the notes aside. Looking back, he found it remarkable that his second and professional Fluentia spell had ended after less than five years. But perhaps one could not impose rules on things that were supposed to happen naturally. What had happened to him was that, returned to his own country, he took up his studies again and in the end produced a doctoral thesis. Nor could one, of course, impose rules on the unforeseen! And yet: could he really not have avoided, at the time, his one great professional disaster? Merten had – then – been utterly convinced that his judgement regarding the most talked about lot in what was probably the Fluentia auction of the century was correct. Now, with hindsight and from a more scholarly viewpoint, he felt somewhat doubtful. But he would have needed to see the statue again – as it was, he only had his memory to go by.

Only a few months after the said auction, he had left. And now, more than ten years later, he was about to go back. He had passed through the ancient city in the meantime, in fact on a couple of occasions – but had never spent more than one or two nights there. But now he was going to give himself a treat: at least a couple of months in the hills near Fluentia! It occurred to him that without his recent and painful surgery, this might never have happened. As the deputy director of a national museum he sometimes even found it difficult to take all his annual leave. Merten, looking across to the small town of Charlottenfels, straightened himself up in his chair. He still felt weak – his heart, however, beat more regularly now than ever before.

He looked at the bundle of papers on the table before him. Suddenly, he thought that maybe his own world was as mad as the world he had tried to depict in his Fluentia diary, all those years past. Only days ago he had read in the local press of a female professor of theology who, having publicly expressed doubts as to whether Mary could after the birth of her son Jesus still be a virgin, lost her university chair – and of the mayor of a town in his, Leander Merten's country, who wanted to increase the height of a nearby mountain: according to maps, this mountain was 4001 metres high when the mayor was still a child, whereas now its height was given as 3998 metres only. God help the man, Merten thought – or rather the volunteers who were to build onto the summit. In his youth, his own nation had always struck him as sadly short of eccentrics. Now he wondered how, given that even here he felt like a spectator in a freak show, he was going to react when again walking through ancient Fluentia. Once more, his thoughts returned to the time of his professional mishap – and to the months which had followed. His recollections made him get up and go for a walk.

4

Interlude: Three Graces and a Dark Lady

He had, after his disaster in the Sirconi sale, decided to lie low for a while. Or at least not to exercise his profession too openly – hence, for the time being, he saw himself as a man of leisure. He knew that in the café, where at the bar he had in the course of only a few weeks become a somewhat familiar figure, they were beginning to wonder about him. Just the other day he had, while ordering his customary drink, overheard two middle-aged ladies: it was claimed, one of them said, that he was a professional gambler. She was distinguished looking, her short hair tinged with grey, and her own comment seemed to arouse rather than repel her. As he remembered the episode, Merten could not help smiling to himself. Let's drink to the man of mystery, he thought – and as the barman put another glass in front of him, it occurred to him that he actually had always had a gambler's instinct. The realization led him right back to the Sirconi sale: why, then, did this instinct not save him! But the next instant, something else captivated both his eye and mind. It was the very latest object of his desire.

As usual she, or the part of her he saw, disappeared again almost immediately. It was all quite photographic: the small, maybe two feet wide opening behind the bar, through which she used to hand snacks to the waiters, serving as a kind of picture frame. Which frame, when she turned around, had just once more highlighted what Merten had become absolutely enthralled with: the most provocative bottom he had ever seen.

Merten drew a deep breath: that he should have become the slave of a Fluentia kitchen-maid! A woman whose name he did not even know – and at a time when he was attempting to reorganize his life and ban all complications from it! For some two weeks he had not had the least idea of what her face looked like. The opening between bar and kitchen was too low. But what buttocks! Eventually, he discovered by chance that whoever went to the lavatory passed the kitchen and saw straight into it. And there she stood: a curvaceous, black-haired woman whose age he found difficult to guess, of medium height and with strong, arched eyebrows. Merten guessed that she came from one of the country towns or villages near Fluentia. She gave him a quick, rather hard look, straightening – she wore a tight black skirt and a thin white blouse – her body at the same time. No doubt the three or four men working around her felt like animals in the circus arena, Merten thought. He remembered a neighbour in the place where he had grown up: a woman of similar aspect and physical attributes, who had buried two husbands in quick succession. Even he, then a mere child, had noticed how the second one grew thinner and thinner … and heard how, even before the man was below the ground, the woman told his father how unlucky she was; adding, with a hard glance, that she still had enough life in her for three fellows. The woman was a nymphet, people in the place said – whatever that meant. A few years later, the boy Leander Frédéric Merten, on the threshold of adolescence, pondered over the expression. It – and the memory of how the woman had looked at his father – caused him shiver-like sensations while he lay awake at night.

Admittedly, the Fluentia kitchen-maid was the younger and more attractive woman. One evening Merten had beheld her in the streets: he spotted her as she left the very place he was about to enter. Obviously she had finished work early.

She wore a pair of close-fitting – he could not help noticing them first – leopard skin trousers and a short black leather jacket. Merten, sidestepping two inquisitive tourists whom nobody seemed to understand, congratulated himself on his quick eye. After pretending to be completely engrossed in the display of a nearby shop window, he followed her round the corner and through the street leading towards the cathedral. At one stage he came so close that, when she abruptly stopped to search her handbag, he almost ran into her. Then, in the throng outside the ancient temple of St. John the Baptist, he lost sight of her. For a while Merten mixed aimlessly with the crowd. Suddenly he caught sight of her again, just as she was about to board a bus. And as she got on, she turned round and – across a dozen or so heads – looked straight at him. He stood transfixed: had she noticed him before, how he followed her? His last vision before the bus doors closed was of her tightly-clad buttocks. For a moment, he was so distracted that he failed to recognize the number of the disappearing bus. But he knew that buses from that stop served two routes which went into the hills north of Fluentia.

Anyway, these were thoughts which went through his head after, on a Friday morning, he had just once more been reduced to playing the part of Peeping Tom. And however intently he stared across the bar: Strange Fruit, as he secretly called it, the posterior which appeared to him like an oversize image of one of those ripe pears he could never resist buying, did not again fill the two feet wide opening. Merten finally raised his eyes to the ceiling, there to find comfort. For the ceiling of the café too was the domain of the female: it was adorned by four rather large frescoes, and in each of these a lady was the undisputed protagonist. What all four had in common was an air of expectancy. It seemed as if they had prepared for an imminent encounter. Probably an amorous encounter – he decided that he, Leander Merten, would happily have obliged any of the four. Why not be a knight in shining armour? Why not Sir Leander – rather than a man suspected of being a professional gambler by some middle-aged gossip! He looked briefly about him – but the two chatterboxes were not present.

Maybe, he wondered, he had been born into the wrong century. It was in fact clear to him whom the frescoed ladies represented – except in the case of one. As to the other three, there were obvious hints: for instance, one lady was being handed an envelope on which the discerning eye could make out the recipient's name. Similarly, in the two pictures that were closest to where he stood the names of two famous ladies - although half-hidden, as if in play - appeared. They were all names of historical persons, women who had lived some four or five hundred years ago. And even the one he still had not managed to identify fitted into the same time frame, Merten felt; a time that was outside his own and to which he yet felt so close. But it was not just the sensuous woman portrayed, it was the picture itself which gave him a headache. It was, in spite of strong similarities in style, so much better than the other three.

He decided he would question the barman, or the man at the till, who seemed to be the boss, about the frescoes. While he still pondered over the mysterious beauty – the painter had surrounded her with putti, flying through the air and tumbling on the floor - he suddenly saw the middle-aged, short-haired woman, the one who took him for a gambler, enter the café. This time she was with another, older companion, a lady with whom Merten was acquainted. The older lady, a countess who was also an artist, had seen him instantly and walked straight up to him. They shook hands. The Countess introduced her female friend, who, as Merten would have expected, was very nosy. Was he married? No!

Then he had to take a local girl, the woman, whose name was Miranda, said without ceremony – adding that the local girls were the most beautiful. To illustrate her claim, she pointed to the fresco above the till. Merten smiled, knowing that the frescoed lady – the one whose name appeared on an envelope – had in fact not been local. The Countess, who knew him well and probably guessed his thought, also smiled. But her short-haired friend kept going on: 'Such a fine-looking man!' she said to the Countess, giving Merten an adoring glance. 'And so young!' Merten, who knew how to handle inquiries of this kind, just laughed good-naturedly. He could foresee the sequel: no doubt she – a surgeon's widow, the Countess had said when presenting her – would before long try to tell him her whole life history.

As it was close to midday and he had an appointment to keep, he finished his drink with an apology and took his leave of the two ladies. When casting a furtive glance in the direction of the counter behind the barman, he was taken by surprise: for the first time, the buxom kitchen-maid had lowered her head and it was her face which appeared in the opening – very obviously to study the scene before her. Was he mistaken? Merten, still flanked by the two older ladies, thought he detected an amused expression in their enigmatic observer's eyes. But abruptly, the kitchen-maid straightened herself and turned round. And in this posture she remained – her buttocks filling the entire opening to bursting point. Thus at least it seemed to Merten; the image was to haunt him for the whole weekend, which he spent away from Fluentia.

★ ★ ★ ★ ★

He lay on a kind of divan, with richly embroidered cloths and tapestry all around him. She bent over him, as if asking for a kiss – and yet, each time he wanted to embrace her, the Duchess withdrew.

Then she motioned him to follow her. He remained inert. But the doorway through which she had stepped seemed to suddenly widen. And thus he saw everything: how a rope descended through the vaulted ceiling above her – and how the villain, pretending to caress her and to readjust her necklace, seized the rope behind her, threw it around her neck and strangled her. When he heard her stifled cry he struggled to get up and reach her, but to no avail …

Merten awoke with a start. Slowly, at first painfully slowly, he was beginning to see things in their right perspective. On his way back to Fluentia on Sunday afternoon, he had come through the hamlet of Greti – and there decided to visit the famous villa. He had stood underneath the ominous hole in the vaulted ceiling of the stately first floor salon and remembered how, on that very spot, the lady who had once been considered the flaming star of Fluentia's most distinguished house ended her life at the hands of her jealous husband. She was less than twenty-four at the time. As her crude executioner, when informing foreign emissaries, put it: she had died 'while washing her hair.'

Later on Monday morning, when he had shaken off his dream, his thoughts drifted back to his by now regular haunt. There, in the café, in one of the frescoes on the ceiling, she was, the at one time flaming star of Fluentia. A lady of letters, an elegant dancer and accomplished musician. A woman, as contemporary sources implied, born to love – and, Merten remembered, an able *equestrienne*. The latter image brought a scene change to his inner eye. 'Strange Fruit!' he sighed, his momentarily blurred mental vision having now assumed the screen-like shape of a certain opening being the domain of a certain kitchen-maid. How he would like to see *that* woman on horseback! Merten decided it was time to get up and … yes, pay a visit to the café.

★ ★ ★ ★ ★

She was not there. Each time something was being pushed through the opening, the arms belonged to one of the men in the kitchen. Suddenly, Merten was angry with himself. After all, he had stopped frequenting his usual drinking places because he needed some kind of an oasis where he could contemplate his professional future. He did not want distraction. So why did he let himself become obsessed with a woman he had, all these weeks, never even spoken a word to? He was beginning to feel depressed. His thoughts turned to another recent episode in his life – a chapter, rather, which was now closed. He should never have let go of the Fandango girl! But the realization had come too late, after she was gone. She had everything he fancied in a woman – and yet, he did not make the slightest effort to persuade her to apply for an extension of her overseas student's grant in order to continue at Fluentia University. Even her name was great: Silvana Fandango. He knew now that the instinct of the celibate had held him back – but it also occurred to him that maybe this had been even bigger a mistake than the one he was to make, shortly after, in the Sirconi sale.

Still standing at the bar, and noticing that nobody in the place had much to do, he decided to ask about the mysterious fresco and the lady in it. The barman shrugged his shoulders – hence Merten walked up to the man at the till, who was indeed the boss. But the boss too did not really know. He claimed, though, that just like in the case of the other ladies – he called them 'graces' – the mysterious beauty's name appeared somewhere in the picture; yet he obviously had been told so by someone else, because he was unable to say exactly where. Nor did he know who the painter, or the painters, of the four ladies had been.

Merten asked for another Armagnac and, glass in hand, positioned himself right underneath the fresco in question.

What also distinguished it from the other three – which were perfectly circular – was its oval shape. Merten's eyes wandered from detail to detail, but to no avail: he could neither detect a name nor the odd letter or two. He paused; then, after another perusal, he walked back to the bar. Only then he noticed the dishevelled fellow sitting in a corner – somebody he knew but did not much care for. Anyway: what on earth had brought this fellow here? No doubt, Merten concluded, the man had seen him study the fresco – after all, the unkempt visitor made a living out of pictures and works of art.

The barman, Merten realized, was eager to talk to him. At the very instant he was taking the orders of some newly arrived guests – but as soon as everybody was served, the man came over.

'About the frescoes,' he said – 'Leo is the one to know.'

He added that he had had a word with the boss; and that most of the café's staff, including the boss and himself, were comparatively new. But that Leo, the oldest waiter, had worked for the previous owner. Merten guessed immediately who Leo was: a waiter of about sixty who obviously dyed his hair, a short, attentive man whose deportment and ways with customers belonged to another era.

'But Leo,' the barman said, 'has his day off work.'

Merten replied that his query was not urgent – but that he was much obliged to the barman and would ask for Leo next time he was here.

When walking through the open door he almost stumbled over one of the pigeons which, from the forecourt, kept at all times invading the place and pestering people who happened to eat a snack. He heard a laugh – and, looking up, beheld the short-haired woman, the surgeon's widow, sitting at one of the tables outside. She beckoned him over.

'Disgusting birds!' she said. There was a pause. 'Although' – she pointed to the café – 'there are people in there far worse. Look at that woman in the kitchen, the one parading her arse!'

Merten was thrilled; hence he accepted happily when she invited him to join her at her table. But as he was about to sit down his eye alighted on the clock on one of the buildings round the square. He realized he was already late for a meeting with a bookseller – which he explained to his new friend, saying he was most chagrined. The surgeon's widow scolded him teasingly; this was the second time, she said, he was running away from her. Anyway, she added with a laugh: she had heard that from time to time he visited the Countess at Fonteluce. Did he know that she lived near the Countess? No?

'Let me give you my address,' she said – adding that she hoped that next time he came to Fonteluce he would, naturally, call on her as well.

'Naturally,' Merten answered, thanking her for her card and telephone number with a slight bow.

Later on this Monday, when on his way home he drove past the so-called Bridge of the Graces, he remembered how the boss in the café had applied the latter word to the three identifiable frescoed ladies. And then he thought of the convent which took its name from an early religious building on this very bridge. Whichever maiden entered this at one time huge convent, Merten recalled, was said to have entered it through a narrow door. Immediately after, the same door was always walled up – it was a symbolic statement for the girls' more or less voluntary isolation from the world.

★ ★ ★ ★ ★

The lady sitting in a cell looked regal. He felt distant – and yet, there he was, alone with her. As he wanted to step up to her, she underwent a sudden transformation: in her place, he beheld a child of eleven, a girl whose eyes talked of danger. Hastily, she started cutting off her hair; then she put on a nun's veil, and in this apparel she seemed strangely composed. But the hordes forcing their way into the convent took her with them. He heard the neighing of horses, then the drumming of hooves – and then the citizens' voices, cheering 'the little nun on horseback.' With heavy legs, he followed. When, from afar, he saw her on her steed, he too wanted to shout. Maybe he had shouted, because at this very moment she turned her head … and changed from veiled child rider to princess and from princess to queen …

His head was aching. However, what shone like jewels in a crown, Merten realized, was no longer a dream image but the sun coming through the blinds. He had, at some stage in the night, fallen asleep on the couch in his study. The books he had collected the previous afternoon were all there, on his desk. While he still lay pondering, he decided to ask his contact the bookseller whether there were any new publications on Fluentia's at one time most powerful family: the one that counted a female who had indeed, in another country, become queen. Merten remembered how she, an orphan a mere fortnight after her birth, had been a political pawn and been moved from city to city and, while in Fluentia, from convent to convent.

She was cultured; but according to the history books not as attractive, Merten recalled, as the ladies who flanked her in the frescoes above the bar in the café. In fact, she was said to have had the protruding eyes and not very fine features of her – nevertheless magnificent – great-grandfather. Only three years after she had been taken by force from the convent where, for ordinary mortals, there was no door back into the world, she was married. Merten's mind returned to the frescoes: only now it occurred to him that another of the four ladies – the one who was being handed a letter – had spent time in the very same convent; she, considered the greatest beauty of her century, had even died there. But who was the fourth lady? Merten remembered the barman's words: that Leo was 'the one to ask.' Intent on this mission, he rose and began to dress.

★ ★ ★ ★ ★

When in the evening he entered the café it occurred to him that he had seen nothing of Strange Fruit since the previous week. Now, back at the bar, he could not see her either – nor the waiter he had come to question. The moment the barman spotted Merten he reached for the Armagnac. But Merten, who, about to leave his place in the morning, had been tempted by the sunshine and spent most of the day reading in his garden, was very thirsty – hence, he shook his head.

'Sparkling wine,' he said; 'provided it's reasonably cool.'

While the barman took a bottle from somewhere and filled his glass, Merten looked around at leisure. It was after seven o'clock, and the place was as busy as a beehive. There was not one face he knew; and since the opening behind the counter did still not reveal Strange Fruit, he started to slowly sip his wine and contemplate the ladies above his head.

'Yes, sir!' a voice in his back said.

Merten, turning round, saw the short elderly waiter stand in front of him.

The barman, obviously the go-between, grinned and gesticulated – 'about the frescoes,' he then said, pointing to the waiter.

'You want to know about the frescoes, sir?' Leo – as always a model of deportment – asked.

It appeared that even Leo knew very little about the frescoed ladies, and nothing as to who had painted them. Yes, he himself had indeed worked for the previous owner, but only after the frescoes had been restored.

'Restored?' Merten was all ears.

Asked whether he knew the restorer's name, the waiter shook his head, looking helpless. 'I am not an educated man, sir,' he added, 'and although I admire these masterpieces it would be presumptuous of me to try and discuss them with you.' Anyway, the proprietor, Leo explained, had never talked much about such matters. At least not to his staff.

Merten had his own view as to what merited the term masterpiece, but he liked the manner of the old waiter; hence he asked whether Leo would care to have a glass of sparkling wine or some other drink on him. The waiter, with a bow, declined immediately, saying that he had to look after his customers. But as he was about to walk off, something arrested him. He looked up to the ceiling, then, pensively, back at Merten. It had just occurred to him, he said after a pause, that years ago when he first worked in the café, a professor came in on various occasions and commented on the fresco. Merten, who with one eye was trying to establish what went on in the kitchen, was momentarily distracted. Was she there, had she even watched him again?

'He commented on the fresco you are interested in, sir,' Leo added with emphasis.

'Yes?' Merten rallied quickly, encouraging Leo with a smile.

The waiter hesitated; he did not know this professor's name, he confessed – 'but he still comes here … although not very often. I think he knew the old owner quite well.'

'Maybe somebody else could help,' Merten suggested, meaning the barman. But he was cut short.

'I can help,' a deep female voice said right next to them.

Leo, who frowned, attempted to brush her aside — but the kitchen-maid stood her ground. Merten felt ecstatic. Before he had a chance to intervene, the woman, dodging the old waiter, bent forward.

'It's Professor Pepalmar Leo is talking about,' she said – 'he lives at Fonteluce.'

And with this she was gone. Merten quickly consulted his watch: it was half past seven, quite some time before the place closed. In fact he did not know when it closed. Not that this mattered very much — what mattered was the time she finished work. 'Tuesday,' he said to himself, 'half past seven.' He watched as the swing door closed behind her fabulous posterior.

Fancy this, he thought – Pepalmar. An archaeologist, not an art historian; but nevertheless the grand old man among Fluentia's scholars. Emeritus professor at the university and – just as important – a good friend of Merten's. Which meant that in this particular moment in time, seven thirty gone on a Tuesday evening, Merten could concentrate on matters other than art.

'A remarkable woman,' he casually said to Leo, indicating with his head the door through which the kitchen-maid had just vanished.

A painful smile passed across the face of the old waiter; but he instantly collected himself. He was glad, he said, if one of them had been of any assistance. Then he excused himself again. 'My customers,' he said — and, after another bow, headed straight for the area with tables where some new guests had sat down.

So she had watched him and listened to what had been said! An impulse urged Merten to follow her – but he checked himself; unless she dallied outside, which was unlikely, the crowds would make it impossible for him to catch up with her. However, he felt in a mood to celebrate and therefore ordered another drink. And then another. For over half an hour he kept reviewing the latest episode and contemplating his next moves. He decided that a visit to Fonteluce was imminent. It occurred to him that he had not seen Pepalmar for over a year; in fact he had heard in the meantime that the professor – aged almost seventy – was intending to get married again. And why not call on the surgeon's widow, Miranda, at the same time? After all, there had been this enigmatic outburst of hers about the woman in the kitchen 'parading her arse.' Merten wondered what she knew. And what would Pepalmar know? Undoubtedly, a talk with the professor would shed some light upon the fresco. And very likely not only that; Pepalmar was a ladies' man – Merten recalled a brief hospital stay of his, and how the professor, who had come to see him, afterwards chased one of the young nurses all over Fluentia. Hence Pepalmar – given the fact that she knew him – would no doubt have something to say about Strange Fruit. Merten, raising his glass, felt almost delirious: never since his recent professional disaster had he been in such high spirits.

Two days later he sat in the square of Fonteluce. His visit was unpremeditated: he had been called to a place some twenty miles north of Fluentia, and on his way back had chosen the more picturesque road leading through the hills – a road which landed him right in the centre of the village. Upon arriving, he had instantly telephoned both Pepalmar and the surgeon's widow, but neither of them was at home; in fact, Pepalmar's answerphone said that the professor was on some excavation site in another country, but would be back before the end of the week. As Merten did not feel like calling upon the Countess, who, as he knew, was wrapped up in pampering a newly divorced, chain-smoking and video-addicted relative, he was about to get into his car again – but then decided to sit down and have a drink instead. And to take in everyday life at Fonteluce; after all, he had once briefly lived here.

'And how is Fluentia's most eminent antiques dealer?'

The question made Merten wince – but he was nevertheless pleased, because he recognized the voice. It belonged to the surgeon's widow, who had stolen up behind him and who – as a mere glance told him – had been out shopping. She had obviously also done her homework on him. He got up and invited her to join him, telling her that he had actually just tried to contact her. She put her shopping bags on one seat and sat down in the other, at the same time calling a nearby waiter and asking for 'the usual thing.' They chatted amicably about nothing in particular until the waiter came back with a coffee and slopped it on the table in front of her. A stain showed on her dress, and Merten was furious – they had always struck him as rude here, he said to her. Indeed they were, she replied, equally annoyed.

Merten was going to avail himself of the incident.

'They are so different where we met, downtown,' he ventured – adding that he liked old-world courtesy. 'Although,' he was quick to continue, 'you seemed to have reservations about someone there. Who again was it – a dish-washer?'

She took the bait immediately. 'That whore in the kitchen,' she yelled; 'the arse woman! Exactly,' she added – 'that woman is beneath contempt.' She bent forward: 'That woman caused the only rift ever between me and my beloved late husband. The woman seduced my husband,' she went on, 'with that big arse of hers! And then he was into all these unnatural practices!'

Merten, who had heard quite enough, tried to calm her down, especially as people at the adjoining tables were becoming their eager audience. Thus he finally learnt that a couple of years earlier the Fluentia kitchen-maid had worked as a cleaner in various Fonteluce households.

'When I employed her, I should of course have asked her about her previous qualifications,' his bereaved companion said with a sneer. As she seemed to get agitated again, Merten changed the subject.

Back in his car, he decided for one more detour before reaching Fluentia. He left Fonteluce in the direction he had come from; then he chose a little road with historical associations, a road which hardly anyone but the older locals seemed to know – but instead of visiting the sanctuary which he had suddenly felt like seeing again, Merten, at a crossroads after some five or six miles, finally followed the sign that pointed towards Fluentia. He consulted his watch: in less than half an hour he would be back in town. And yet, out where he still was he always felt in another world. Somewhere nearby, it was believed, there had been a *curtis* – the seat of an ancient court. While his car took the downhill bends almost effortlessly, Merten let his eyes roam across the dramatic landscape. Eventually, near the bottom of the valley, the castle came in sight: the place where, as tradition would have it, the attempted overthrow of Fluentia's mightiest family had once been plotted.

★ ★ ★ ★ ★

He walked along the road to the castle – but somehow, he seemed rooted. The lady who had overtaken him, hand in hand with a little boy, passed him again on her way back. This time she was alone. Struck by her beauty, he turned round. But somebody had waited for her: a woman in the habit of a religious order. A horse-drawn carriage emerged from underneath the trees. The moment she lifted – aided by the nun – her foot to board the carriage, he recognized her. He wanted to run, to be with her; after all, nobody had come to her help when a whole town under her command had been besieged by a wicked pope's villainous son. The images in his head started melting into one another. Suddenly, he himself sat in a carriage. He was on his own, and he shouted to the coachman to make haste. The carriage stopped, and he stepped out into a square. And there she was, high up on a balcony: younger than just before and dressed in brown velvet – but underneath her mantle he could see a coat of arms. Three times widowed she was, at only thirty-six. In order to see her better, he stepped backwards. He struck against something – it was a draw-well. Here, in this same town, her first husband had been pushed out of a window by assassins. Looking down into the murky water, he shuddered. Her revenge was said to have been terrible: cisterns and wells full of mangled bodies. And up there she still was; another city had opened its gates to the pope's villainous son the way a whore would open her legs, but she, the lady in chain mail, was determined to fight to the last. When the arrows started to whizz over his head, he flung himself to the ground ...

The noise was caused by torrential rain. Merten, rubbing his eyes, realized that it was still night – but he did not want to go back to sleep. Numbly, he groped for the light switch. The sequel to the story was horrible, he thought. After the outbreak of a fire within the fortress, she had had to surrender unconditionally; and, abused by the victor, was to spend sixteen months in a dungeon. Even after her liberation – a foreign monarch had interceded on her behalf – she had to use detours while travelling towards Fluentia, the home of her late third husband. To be evil was her enemy's motto - hence his murderous bloodhounds could lie in ambush anywhere. She did arrive safely, though; and, before dying seven years later, saw her little son grow up happily in the vicinity of the city. The lad was said to be a fine horseman when he was just over six – obviously he took after his noble mother, one of whose ancestors had distinguished himself as a soldier of fortune.

Merten was trying to visualize the fresco in the café. No doubt it was her: the lady who was given an envelope. He knew that she had not been particularly learned – but what a woman! A beauty with a great heart and great courage; he would at any time have taken his hat off to her. But who was the other one? The thought of the fourth lady was beginning to drive him mad. Very sensuous she seemed; and beautiful too – but admittedly, there was a touch of vulgarity. Or was it only his imagination? And then there was the picture as such: whatever his uncertainties as to the woman portrayed, this fourth fresco was a work of art, whereas the others were not. Merten decided that for a week or so he would just concentrate on the said work – Strange Fruit could wait. He realized that, when in Fonteluce, he had not even asked what her name was. But of course he quite relished the terminology the surgeon's widow employed when referring to her at one time rival! Anyway, one thing, he promised himself, had to take precedence: he had to catch hold of Pepalmar and fathom the professor's memory about the restoration of the frescoes all those years ago. He realized – not without pleasure – that suddenly his professional drive was reasserting itself.

★ ★ ★ ★ ★

It was Saturday, just before noon. Merten, having parked on the road above, immediately spotted Pepalmar in his garden. But the latter had seen him too.

'I see you are taking professional mishaps very seriously!' Pepalmar shouted; then, with his typical musical laugh, he ascended the stairs and came to the gate. Merten gave the professor a questioning look.

'You are in mourning, Leander,' Pepalmar said teasingly, 'and this on a fine summer day.'

Merten smiled. Of course Pepalmar knew that black was his favourite colour. And although he was not surprised that news of his recent flop had travelled as far as here, he experienced a feeling of relief at the professor's jocular hint. There was at times a touch of almost fatherly concern coming from Pepalmar; at least, Merten thought, he had always been free to speak his mind here – and, what was more important, he felt understood by the older man.

Pepalmar had prepared a light lunch, which he said he would serve in the garden. First, however, he wanted to know what exactly it was Merten – who on the telephone had only briefly mentioned the café and the frescoes – wanted to question him about. Hence, as they sat down, Merten came straight to the point. He told Pepalmar of his visits to the café and of his – he paused, and then laughed as he continued – 'special relationship' with the frescoed ladies; and also that it was mentioned to him that he, Pepalmar, had years ago been called in to give his opinion re the one picture that was undoubtedly superior to the others. So who was the painter, who the restorer – and whom was the lady supposed to represent?

The professor nodded. Yes, he said, he remembered very well how the previous owner kept pestering him.

'You know, he had some old relatives who had more than once told him that one of the frescoes in the place was by a famous old master. But then, suddenly, these relatives were dead – and nobody else in the owner's family knew much about either the frescoes or the history of both building and café. And as you know very well this is not exactly my field,' Pepalmar continued; 'hence, I am afraid I cannot enlighten you.'

Merten wanted to know about the restorer: what did the restorer think? Hadn't Pepalmar met him? The professor shook his head. Merten's informant must have got the sequence of events wrong or rushed to conclusions. The frescoes had been restored before he, Pepalmar, first set foot in the place. In other words: the old owner had never even told him who the restorer was.

'But,' the professor said, 'I agree with you: the picture you are interested in is better than the others.' He also agreed with Merten as to who the other three ladies were. The fourth one? Pepalmar admitted he had no clue. 'Just rack your brains, Leander,' he then added with a quick laugh; 'I am sure it's worth it – after all, you are in pursuit of a beauty ....'

While Pepalmar walked back to the house to, as he said, concentrate on the gastronomical part of their meeting, Merten relaxed. The air in the garden – the whole hillside above Fonteluce being a kind of forest – was intoxicating. Suddenly, hell broke loose in the trees above him. 'Goddamned cats!' the professor shouted from the house, before Merten even had a chance to establish what was going on. But then he saw what was happening: about thirty feet above him, one cat chased another. In the style of jet-fighters, the two animals raced from treetop to treetop. He had never witnessed anything like it.

Pepalmar, who now emerged from the house with cold meat and wine, was still cursing. His fiancée, he said, had gone to see her mother over the weekend and asked him to look after her cat – a despicable cat, he added, an animal that had never seen a tree before and was accustomed to velvet cushions and pink salmon. Merten smiled, knowing that Pepalmar hated animals.

'And the other, the aggressive one, is yours, of course,' Pepalmar shouted in despair - 'that stray cat you used to feed!'

At this stage, Merten could not help laughing aloud. When nearly seven years ago, very briefly, he had been Pepalmar's neighbour, he had a visitor one morning. First, he only saw two paws – then the head of a very young tiger-cat appeared, surveying his lounge through the glass door, from outside. The intruder was injured, probably after a fight. In the weeks that followed, the animal became one of his best friends ever. So up there she was, he thought, leaning back once more and trying to absorb the whole incredible treetop landscape which in the sun looked like filigree against a dark blue sky.

After his host had, in the course of lunch, reeled off the latest news and extolled the qualities of his fiancée with considerable relish – at forty-seven she had 'the body of a teenager' – , Merten brought up the café again. He told the professor who had been his source there.

'Ah, the kitchen-maid!' Pepalmar exclaimed approvingly and looked Merten full in the face – 'you like her, don't you?' he then added with his quick laugh. He did not even wait for a reply. Years ago, as a girl, she had been a real stunner and was much talked about, the professor went on – but then her marriage started going wrong. Merten raised his eyebrows. 'Oh, yes,' Pepalmar affirmed; 'it was said that in the end she even walked the streets for a while, her husband who was much older acting as her pimp. Then, one day, her father stepped in – and since, unless things changed, she has been living at the old man's place.'

No, he did not know who her ex-husband was, Pepalmar said in answer to Merten's question – 'but reportedly a violent fellow, somebody who kept clashing with the law. Her father, by the way, arranged for her to have that job in the café.' Pepalmar nodded emphatically, aware that his visitor had not expected so much background detail; yes, her father was a waiter in the café, he then explained.

Merten remembered instantly: how Leo tried to stop her when she stepped between them. And also how the old waiter smiled painfully when afterwards he, Merten, attempted to change the subject and talk about her. 'What is her name?' he asked Pepalmar.

The Professor looked perplexed: 'You know, I can't even remember!' He searched his memory. 'No, I can't tell you,' he added after a while – he said he seemed to remember, though, that it was not her real name which people used to call her by.

Merten concluded, without telling the professor, that for the moment he did not really need to know her name – that "Strange Fruit" as a label was still good enough for him. After all, not everyone had a name as fine and fitting as the Fandango girl. The sudden memory of someone who was now irrevocably beyond his reach made him wince. He was surprised to notice that he hoped Pepalmar, who had declared himself to be a great admirer of La Fandango, would not ask about how he, Merten, had taken her departure.

'So what was all this talk about, Leander?' Pepalmar wanted to know after a little while; 'this talk about your role in the Sirconi sale?'

Merten, although initially prepared for the question, had to first clear his mental vision – heat, wine and impressions past and present, everything suddenly interacting.

'Did you really believe your opinion to be correct?' Pepalmar asked gently.

'Yes' – Merten, whose recent misfortune it had been to apparently misattribute a statue in the said Fluentia auction, slowly indicated his firm conviction. Consulted by the auction house, he had declared the statue – a Cupid without wings – to be almost five hundred years old. 'I based my judgement not only on style, but also on the well-known tradition that at that time two such statues embellished the fountain in the garden of the Grand Duke's villa at –'

'But that fountain is of an even earlier date,' Pepalmar broke in.

'Of course,' Merten conceded – 'the fountain, yes; but not necessarily the said statues.' He added that he had been careful to further support his claim by referring to a letter which the man he took for the sculptor had written to his father, mentioning a "figure" the Grand Duke had commissioned from him. But anyhow, the statue did not sell – and since due to this particular lot the event had been styled the sale of the century, the media had been quick to enlist some of Merten's enemies and pour scorn on, as they put it, a money-making dealer's expertise. He admitted that his mistake was not to have recommended a more conservative estimate to the auction house; he should have known that it was this, in other words the whole hype, which would help mobilize the opposition.

Suddenly, Pepalmar started laughing. 'The God of Love!' he exclaimed – 'what else but trickery can you expect from him?' As the God of Love the statue had for some weeks made headlines in the press. Merten, as always when the professor had one of his fits of mirth, could not help being amused. 'Maybe you should stay clear of him, Leander,' Pepalmar warned; 'I mean, let's forget about the wretched sale' – he now shook with laughter – 'but don't confuse love with your obvious interest in that kitchen-maid's bum.'

An hour later, Merten was on the road to Fonteluce and from there to Fluentia. His thoughts returned to the auction, to what – in connection with it – bothered him more than his dented reputation. The man who many years before had sold the statue to its present owner was a junk dealer. What he had got was peanuts – and when he heard, on television, what the statue was expected to fetch in the so-called sale of the century, this man died of a heart attack. Merten had deliberately kept quiet about the episode at Pepalmar's, guessing that perhaps the professor did not know. Very likely, however, Pepalmar would have made light of the matter – he would have called the man a silly bugger or something, thus dismissing the whole affair. After a while, Merten in his car did likewise: he banished all thoughts of the Sirconi sale.

★ ★ ★ ★ ★

When the day after he entered the café, the Countess stood at the bar.

First, her conversation was as elegant as ever. She then casually mentioned having heard of his visits to Fonteluce, acknowledging the surgeon's widow as her source of information – 'You know,' she added, 'my friend has taken quite a shine to you.' But thereupon, her voice changed. 'Keep your distance,' she warned coldly, 'that woman is just a randy bitch. And a gossip too!' Merten, who had never heard her use such language, was quite taken aback. 'It's Miranda I mean,' she emphasized: 'the surgeon's widow.' Having followed his eyes, which for a moment only had gone astray, the Countess laughed. 'Yes,' she said, indicating the kitchen: 'undoubtedly you heard "her story" through Miranda.' Merten wanted to feign ignorance, but she was too fast. 'There is a sequel to that story,' she went on; 'our friend the widow screws with the kitchen-maid's lowly ex-husband.'

He decided that their meeting was a rewarding one. Hence he suggested sitting down at one of the tables outside to the Countess.

Leo, who stood in the open door and whom Merten had not seen, lashed out wildly – 'the pigeons,' the waiter said, bowing and then stepping aside to let the Countess and Merten pass.

Merten helped the Countess to a chair in the shade. Having sat down himself, he vaguely pointed in the direction of the kitchen. 'How come that you know her?' he inquired.

'I shared her with Miranda,' the Countess replied, adding that the woman had cleaned both the house of the surgeon's widow and her own place for a while.

'And am I to understand that her husband was for hire, too?' Merten asked with an amused smile.

The Countess laughed – 'No,' she said, explaining that when the kitchen-maid first worked at Fonteluce, the fellow never even showed up. She had left him before, and they all understood she lived at some elderly relative's. 'But then, suddenly, he seemed to miss her and started spying on her. He was reported not just to be a very rough individual, but also something of a sex maniac - qualities that cannot fail to impress Miranda, who was married to the most boring man!' The Countess obviously savoured her words. However, checking herself she admitted that the affair between this undaunted individual and the surgeon's widow seemed to be quite new: the two had recently, on more than one occasion, been seen in the hills around Fonteluce.

'In the hills?' Merten asked.

The Countess, who could not help pausing for effect, nodded – 'yes,' she finally continued, 'screwing in that little car of hers.'

Somebody bent over their table. It was Leo – apologizing for the interruption and asking whether they intended to order another drink. After they had done so, and after the waiter had left, the Countess was the first to speak again.

'I believe this old geezer is quite keen on our buxom friend,' she said, adding that she had seen waiter and kitchen-maid go to the bus stop together, with the old man carrying her shopping bags. She laughed – 'Why not: as a pair, they seem better suited than a surgeon's widow and a journeyman … or whatever that fellow is!'

Merten remained silent; as she obviously did not know, he was not going to give away what he had learnt about "the pair" at Pepalmar's. However, he wanted to ask her where Strange Fruit – he had to check himself – where the buxom one was supposed to live with, as she had put it, some elderly relative. But the Countess was pondering over something.

'She called him in to do a job,' she suddenly said.

'Who?' Merten asked; 'who called whom?'

The Countess looked lost; 'Miranda,' she then said, abruptly. 'Miranda asked that woman's ex to do a job in the house, something the woman had said he was good at. This must have been the beginning of their *liaison*.' He saw that her temperament was about to get the better of her. But, admirably, she held back; 'no doubt Miranda,' she just added, 'made it very easy for him.'

When Leo put their drinks in front of them, Merten remembered that already the previous week he had wanted to contact his bookseller friend. He asked the Countess to excuse him for a moment – telling her that he had to make a long due telephone call. Inside the building, he paused underneath the mysterious fresco; yes, he thought, definitely an interesting picture. He had to once more admit to himself, though, that something about it seemed rather crude – but again he could not quite say what. The composition was fine; so was it perhaps the painter's – or restorer's – execution of some detail? Or was it the protagonist of the picture herself? Whatever the answer, he felt positive that a talk with his bookseller contact would help him a step further in his search.

Having made his telephone call – the bookseller indeed had an old tome on the great ladies of Fluentia, which he said he would put aside – Merten was puzzled to see the very same unkempt fellow who had once before watched him study the fresco. Again it was unmistakable that the man had seen him. This one had his eyes everywhere, Merten thought … just as when, some two years ago, he had called on Merten, offering his services. 'For odd jobs,' he had said – adding that he had a knowledge of both art and antiques. The fellow probably still felt resentful at having been given rather short shrift at the time. But being an aesthete, Merten had little time for the ungainly; hence even this time he forgot the man almost the moment he saw him. In fact, something else arrested him as he was about to walk through the swing door: it was the realization that he had, while using the telephone next to the kitchen, not even checked whether Strange Fruit was there.

★ ★ ★ ★ ★

It was early in the evening, the day after. Merten walked across the square in front of St. John the Baptist. He had just been at his bookseller's – and somehow it seemed too late to do something else, but too early to go home. So he went to the café and walked up to the bar. From the opening to the kitchen, which was temporarily empty, his eyes wandered up to the ceiling. He felt unusually relaxed, and true to the spirit of the moment, the frescoed ladies appeared to him like secret allies: the one sitting on some kind of sarcophagus in a bower, being handed an envelope – and next to this fair warrior and greatest beauty of her age the one who was to become queen in another country, she semi-reclined in a boudoir, her name appearing on a small, urn-like vessel which might have contained her toiletry. More to the left, the at one time pride of Fluentia: murdered by a jealous husband and here depicted by an unknown painter within an arched wooden frame, very likely a lover's haunt in some ornamental garden. One, of course, remained elusive: she – he walked over to the corner right underneath the fresco – a woman surrounded by putti flying through the air and tumbling on the floor. He spontaneously decided to call her his Dark Lady.

Suddenly, Merten felt intrigued. He had a closer look. It seemed to him that something in the picture had changed – if hard pressed, he would have said something about her hair. But what exactly? He could not be sure, and hence dismissed the whole thing as a figment of his imagination. He walked back to the bar to look out, as he said to himself, for a shape more substantial.

Strange Fruit was there, but for once revealed very little of herself through the opening. After a while, his thoughts having returned to the frescoes, Merten decided to go and sit down at one of the tables outside. Given, he reflected while making himself comfortable there, that the other three were women whose names appeared in every history of Fluentia: would it not follow that the fourth one, his Dark Lady, was somehow related to them? He let the other three pass in front of his mental eye: was there any obvious connection he just did not see? The book he was reading at home and would have to return soon had not yet supplied him with a clue. But then, he thought, he was probably too fascinated with a single story in it – the story of one who had come to Fluentia as a fallen woman.

★ ★ ★ ★ ★

The next day, a Thursday, he spent mainly with the book he had borrowed – and when he got up on Friday, it was with the intention of going to a museum he had not visited for over a year. He wanted to look at a certain portrait which hung there.

A few hours later, Merten was on his way from the museum to the café. The portrait, he had to admit to himself, had been somewhat disappointing. Not disappointing as a work of art, being after all in the style of a well-known Fluentia school; but not the kind of face he felt was appropriate for the woman – not only a fallen woman, but an adventuress – he had become engrossed with in the course of his recent reading.

With these thoughts he entered the café. He only wanted a quick drink; but he was rewarded with one of the most provocative sights ever of Strange Fruit. Had she seen him come in? Was this a deliberate act of hers? His own wishful thinking amused him. Having emptied his glass at one draught and ready to leave, he raised his eyes and cast a brief glance at the fresco above the corner table. He was stunned. Was his famous photographic memory – famous at least before a wingless Cupid led him up the garden path in the Sirconi sale – letting him down? He could have sworn that his Dark Lady was portrayed with reddish hair; whereas – he walked closer – the fresco quite clearly showed her with dark brown hair. Quite in keeping, he thought, with his newly coined name for her. She also seemed more voluptuous than before – although she had always struck him as generously proportioned.

★ ★ ★ ★ ★

He waited down in the dark street right opposite her house, having some intelligence for the Prince. In church he had seen how His Highness feasted his eyes on her – hence he had no doubt that the Prince would pay her a visit. He looked up to the illuminated open window, from which strange and enticing vapours emanated. Was it true that, as people said, she had ensnared Fluentia's most powerful man by practising magic and having recourse to love potions? Suddenly he saw her cross the room – and then he recognized the Prince who, from the other side, stepped up to her. Locked in an embrace, they disappeared from sight. So there really was an underground passage, connecting the nearby ducal palace with her house! While he mused on this and other popular rumours, he heard screams from the direction of the river. Although nobody could be seen, he knew instantly what was happening: a band of hired assassins had finally caught up with her husband. The screams came closer. Again he knew what it meant. Her husband had managed to escape his assailants – but when about to enter his house hurriedly through a back door near the church of the Holy Spirit, he was intercepted by some others who had been lying in ambush there and were presently joined by their churlish allies. Their victim was a skilled swordsman, but there were too many of them. What followed was a massacre. An accidental witness, he looked up to the illuminated window from where strange odours still poured forth; somewhere in that muted light, the lovemaking between the murdered man's wife and the Prince went on undisturbed …

The screams had been the vocal manifestations of an itinerant wine merchant who often woke him early in the morning. Soaked in his sheets, Merten cursed the man – coming in with his cart from the wine-producing region south of Fluentia, this merchant had the tendency to make a halt right outside his gallery, above which he had his lodgings.

When the merchant went quiet and moved on, Merten's mind returned to the dream sequence. It struck him as strange that he had not seen the woman's face – and yet, hers was the story of the adventuress in the book. Was she faceless in his dream because he could not accept that hers had been the features of the woman in the portrait at the museum? Perhaps. He thought of her reputation as a sorceress – surely a lot of it was total rubbish. After all, there were sources according to which her husband – who had raped her when she was only sixteen and made her flee her native city – had in the hope of preferment even urged her to succumb to the Prince's advances. A vain, despicable opportunist, Merten thought. Yet, he had to give him his due: in his last stand against a horde far more despicable, this man had displayed great courage.

★ ★ ★ ★ ★

The same morning Merten had to return the book. When he entered his acquaintance the bookseller's place, he saw an empty dustjacket on the desk next to the entrance. The jacket belonged to the book he was carrying with him. But it was not this fact as such which gave him a thrill: it was the face of the woman on the cover.

The bookseller, who emerged from a back room, followed his eye. 'It's torn,' he said apologetically; 'that's why I kept it here – I'll have to mend it with some tape.'

Merten paid little attention to the man's words. As he took the cover, his hands trembled slightly – the shake, he knew, heralded a discovery which at the same time would be a personal triumph. He walked over to the window. 'Samira, mistress of the second Grand Duke of Fluentia,' he read inside the flyleaf – 'detail of a fresco believed to be 16th century.' His heart pounded, then missed a few beats: the woman he had read – and dreamed – about, the one shown on the dustjacket in his hands, was the woman in the fourth fresco on the ceiling of the café! He should have come to this conclusion before, as the said Samira had had a friend in the Grand Duke's sister … who was the murdered Duchess in the fresco right next to his now identified Dark Lady. Only one thing disturbed him: the woman on the cover had reddish hair, looked, in other words, the way the fresco had imprinted itself in his mind – whereas at the time of his last visit to the café there was no doubt about the frescoed lady's dark brown hair. The painful memory of his recent professional flop came back to him. Maybe he was kidding himself? Or did he perhaps have to go to an oculist? Merten decided to verify the matter without delay; knowing that there was a place nearby where he could have colour photocopies made, he asked the bookseller whether he might borrow the dustjacket for a few minutes.

Not much later the same day, he arrived at the café, carrying his photocopy of Samira the Grand Duke's consort with him. He walked up to the bar, ordered a large Armagnac, took a sip and then went straight over to the corner underneath the fourth fresco. Yes, he could still rely on his photographic memory! The resemblance between the lady on the book cover and the lady in the fresco was unmistakable. However, he also noticed that the frescoed lady's hair, which last time he thought had changed from reddish to dark brown, was now almost black. Which meant that someone kept changing the picture! Merten, rooted to the spot underneath the fresco, was at a loss. Eventually, he walked back to the bar to finish his drink. Whoever was responsible for the trickery: he concluded that this fraud was not a gifted artist. In the beginning, in spite of his minor reservations, it had seemed obvious that the fresco was by a master – now with the changes, Merten judged it only marginally better than the three other works which kept it company.

5

Last Stop Down Memory Lane

The eve of departure had come. Merten, in his ancestral home near the small town of Charlottenfels, once more pondered over the events which had put an end to his early professional spell in Fluentia. Pulled to pieces by the media, he had lost credibility – and as his attempt at making a living as an art and antiques dealer there had been more or less coincidental, he had eventually come to the conclusion that the time for a move was right. Mindful of his abandoned studies and early university prize, he had felt that glory was worth another attempt. Why should he allow himself to be humiliated by a crowd that was typical not only of modern Fluentia, but of an entire country: an egocentric, ill-advised, shallow lot? And yet, on the terrace of his ancestral home near Charlottenfels, Merten concluded that he had always – and still – loved the Fluentia way of life.

He thought of his few visits to the ancient city in the ten or so intervening years; and of how he had, on each occasion, gone back to the café. The first time – only about six months after he had left – he instinctively looked out for Strange Fruit. She was not there. However, when he paid his respects to the four ladies on the ceiling, he made a startling discovery. His at one time Dark Lady looked the way he remembered the kitchen-maid – the abundant black hair, the ample curves: it was her! Just as he had assumed before he left, he was tempted to believe that somebody must have made changes to the fresco. Or had he simply not noticed the likeness before? Merten, no longer a resident of Fluentia, felt most intrigued.

Then, there was his second visit. And two or three subsequent ones. When he returned for the second time, some two years had passed – but the kitchen-maid was there. She even came out and helped the barman; however, it seemed she did not recognize him. Perhaps she just did not see him, as he had already been served and stood slightly apart. Merten studied her unobtrusively for a while. She was younger than he had always thought; he decided that, very likely, her often rather hard facial expression had deceived him – and Pepalmar's comments had probably misled him too. But of course the professor, although at the time about to marry a middle-aged woman, was notoriously attracted to young girls barely past the age of puberty. When she disappeared into the kitchen, his eyes once again turned to the ladies portrayed on the ceiling. What he beheld made him question his faculties more than ever: his Dark Lady had reddish hair again. Incredulous, Merten walked over to the corner underneath the fresco. Yes, indeed – and with the reddish hair, the likeness to Strange Fruit was gone. On his two or three subsequent visits, the fresco looked the same. And not only was the likeness to Strange Fruit gone; Merten had since then never caught sight of the kitchen-maid again.

One last time before retiring for the night, he walked to the extremity of the terrace and looked across to the lights of Charlottenfels. He heard a train go into the tunnel which passed through the rock underneath his ancestral home. Merten remembered how, in his early childhood, these trains were still being pulled by steam locomotives. As the locomotives had to negotiate a considerable gradient, the noise, at night, had always been somewhat eerie – it was like hearing, from somewhere deep inside the earth, a giant bring an equally gigantic hammer down on an anvil. Again and again, in quick succession. He lingered for a while. It struck him that the metaphor was quite apt; after all, the landscape some fifteen miles to the east of Charlottenfels was littered with long-extinct volcanoes.

Finally, with everything around him silent again, he became aware of another acoustic component of his childhood. A murmur only, heard from where he was – although a thundering inferno at the spot it originated from. He had been down there in the afternoon and gazed into the colour disk of the vaporizing water. The falls were said to be over 17,000 years old. Not only much older, but somehow far more mysterious than ancient Fluentia, he thought. A bell from the village on the other side of the river reminded him of the hour – and with his journey once more on his mind, Merten stepped back into the house and closed the doors to the terrace behind him.

6

Fluentia Re-visited

Alas, that was a long time ago! He had just reread his Fonteluce notes, which he had unearthed whilst recuperating in his native place. And now, here he was again: in the hills north of Fluentia … The whole landscape felt very ancient, and cobwebs in some of the rooms – he had rented an old villa – added to this sense of timelessness. The next day, a woman from a nearby village was to present herself, as he had made it known before his arrival that he needed a housekeeper. Anyway, the hamlet of Opaco, in which an isolated church seemed the only other building of note, suited him ideally: from here to Fluentia it was barely half an hour's drive.

A long time ago – and yet: when in the morning he had passed through Fonteluce, everything seemed so familiar. He felt that even where the road narrowed most dangerously, he could have closed his eyes – it was like magic, the steering wheel just doing everything right. First, the sight of some buildings brought back memories. The dentist's house, for instance: with shutters closed, like all those years ago. He was wondering whether the family were still sitting in there in complete darkness, and whether the eldest daughter still ate nothing but rice. And was the dentist still given to hitting patients who refused to hold a mirror whilst he operated on them?

When he briefly parked his car and got out, he found himself suddenly – and most uncannily – surrounded by the old Fonteluce crowd. To begin with, that horrible George was still selling newspapers in the square. Merten also recognized the man at the gas station – who was balding very fast now. And then the dark-haired girl – maybe the term woman was more appropriate, but she still looked young – at the cash counter of the little supermarket. Even an employee in the bank looked familiar. And of course the so-called persons of authority here still grovelled before you if you knew somebody with a big name! Thus, when he was greeted by a well-connected lady whom he had not expected to see right upon his arrival – when this lady, none other but the Countess, embraced him, the marshal, who had started to move threateningly towards his car, almost fell over in the attempt of bowing and scraping. He had in fact always disliked this man – a creep who, needless to say, did not recognize him – intensely. Merten felt that, very likely, he would at some stage want to do something to the marshal.

So here he was – sitting in the garden of a grand old house at Opaco and trying to pigeonhole the impressions of a man on the threshold of a *recherche du temps perdu*. The fact was: he had not yet been down to Fluentia. Apart from arriving with the airport train, of course – however, outside the railway station he had taken a taxi and made straight for the hills. But he was fortifying himself against the Fluentia experience. Somehow, he just wanted to keep sitting in the garden at Opaco. The distant, frequent ringing of bells – it came from a monastery high up on the hillside – was very soothing. Yet, he decided to visit Fluentia the next day. In two days, that is; he had to remind himself that seeing the local woman who, hopefully, would prove suitable as a housekeeper took absolute priority.

He suddenly felt very tired. The air was intoxicating. Some dry meat, cheese, grapes and red wine, he decided, would be perfect for dinner. With this objective, he went back into the villa. In spite of the numbness of his brain, he knew he was likely to revive in a couple of hours – he had never been a man to go to bed early. Hence, whilst preparing his meal, he also looked for candles. No doubt he would later be sitting in the garden again; before he retired for the night, he wanted to witness nature go to sleep. What a treat: to be out there and hear this ancient landscape fall silent.

★ ★ ★ ★ ★

Years ago, a great writer was the guest of my parents at Charlottenfels. He had just been shortlisted for a most prestigious literary prize – but he had also come under fire from some of the luminaries of literary criticism. He was, they claimed, too obsessed in his writings with the events which had shaped his own life. I asked him whether he thought his detractors had a point. He smiled, but did not answer. I rephrased my question: I said I had detected a lot of autobiographical detail in his early writings – but how important were personal experiences for a mature practitioner in the art of letters? He deliberated for a moment. 'There are always experiences which leave you bewildered, Leander,' he then said; 'and you write about them in an attempt to get a grip on them.'

Today, in my garden at Opaco, I decided that these words should be the kick-off to a new, albeit occasional diary of mine. The fact is: there are things here which already puzzle me greatly. And had I not, when recuperating at Charlottenfels, contemplated starting a diary again? But perhaps I should, before going into details, say a few words about the place. The villa I have rented is situated above the main road, which at one time was a pilgrim's route. At the end of a driveway, it is shielded by a semi-circle of farmhouses. This complex of buildings is in fact a winemaking co-operative. Hence, there is a steward here – who is also my main contact, as I have not yet met, nor even caught the name of, the owner of the villa. Anyway, it is my meeting with the steward this morning which suddenly prompted me to take up the pen.

The steward, whose name is Gastone, originates from the plains near the sea – which are the home of some of the finest horsemen this region has ever produced. Gastone had actually just been visiting relatives there over the weekend. And what – in the late 20th century! – was his experience? Gastone tells me that the whole commune he comes from is held spellbound by a sorcerer. Apparently, the people have discovered strange signs – like pebbles, arranged in a certain way – in nearby forests. Consequently, they go out there in groups, especially the young and always in the early evening, 'in pursuit of the sorcerer.' Gastone, who on one occasion joined them, swears that he even saw the creature – but then, he says, he heard a sound as if a door was closing, and the apparition was gone. When I questioned him, he readily admitted that within a radius of some two or three kilometres there was no house, hut or other dwelling. Nevertheless, it seems that even the press believe in this nonsensical affair – according to Gastone, there were various journalists amongst the party in pursuit of the sorcerer.

And this is the country of which I once believed that only here a man could still – and truly – be a Renaissance man! Yet, compared to what was to follow in the afternoon, my interview with Gastone, in other words his tale, must seem almost reasonable.

In the afternoon I walked down to the main road, from where it is only a stone's throw to the isolated little church of Opaco. This church, by the way, occupies the very site of what is said to have been the court of Alpiniano. But who Alpiniano was, or when a nobleman with such a name might have lived, not even the locals have the slightest idea.

Anyway, whilst there I got engaged in conversation with the sacristan. Once again, from on high, the bells of the monastery *rang out — and as I stood listening, the sacristan, whose approach I had not noticed, started talking about the weeping madonna. First I took the man for a harmless lunatic. But then, seeing that I was a stranger, he introduced himself. He was amazed, though, he said, at my not having heard of the statue in the village underneath the monastery — which statue has reportedly been weeping blood since Candlemas. I was equally amazed, of course; I even admitted it, pointing at the same time to the old villa across the road and identifying myself as its new occupant. The sacristan, who seemed to view me favourably as a neighbour, raised an eyebrow. 'But these winemaking people over there are heathens, sir,' he said, thus excusing my ignorance.*

The said madonna, I then learnt, is a small statue which until recently stood in the garden of a villager — a souvenir the latter brought back from a visit to some country now torn apart by civil war. Suddenly, on Candlemas day, a little girl saw red tears on the statue's face: the madonna had wept blood. The girl told her father, her father told the priest, and the priest told his superiors. And of course the villagers also spread the news — after all, the miraculous weeping was to continue! Soon, sensation seekers started to arrive from elsewhere; and this was when, according to my informant, the priest took the madonna into his custody.

However, when the abbot of the monastery above the village went on television, declaring in a programme broadcast nationwide that the madonna had wept in his very presence, the die was cast. Overnight the village became — as it had been in its heyday — a centre of pilgrimage. And now, Easter is at hand. Expecting the faithful in thousands, abbot and priest not only made arrangements for wheelchair access and mobile toilets: they insisted that the madonna be placed behind bulletproof glass in a niche in the parish church. On the road underneath the village — the same road which farther down the valley, at Opaco, passes my villa — somebody set up a stall with replicas of the madonna.

What a story, what a place! I was just going to make a polite comment to this effect, but the sacristan raised his hand, thus indicating that he had not yet finished. There was an afterword, he said — although no doubt only a provisional one. This provisional afterword belongs to the mayor of the place: a man who, I discovered quickly, is a communist and an atheist. So what did the mayor do? He arranged that the madonna, rather than being placed behind bulletproof glass, was confiscated by the district attorney. And not only this; suspecting a mechanism inside, mayor and district attorney had the statue X-rayed and further tested at Fluentia University. Although their suspicion proved to be unfounded, they were to triumph: the tears the madonna had wept, the university's scientists claim, are the blood not of a woman but of a man. Needless to say that now the blood of the villager in whose garden the madonna shed her first tears is to be examined. Who can blame the nuns in a nearby convent for having gone berserk when the news reached them?

And what — if the scientists are right — about the thousands expected here for Easter? But this is a rhetorical question. I already knew before my return that this country, traditionally the prey of the most abominable political careerists, is in deep trouble. The people yearn for a change — and a miracle, as both mayor and central government must know, is bound to be taken as a signal for better times by the blindfolded multitudes.

Maybe, as tomorrow is Good Friday, I shall further postpone my going down to Fluentia. As I have always been interested in the festivities which are staged there on Holy Saturday, it seems worthwhile to wait. And perhaps it would be fun to join the crowds who tomorrow, unfailingly, will be looking for the weeping madonna up in the village? Before or after my outing, I could even continue this diary. After all, the local woman who presented herself today and offered her services as a housekeeper deserves a mention too.

★ ★ ★ ★ ★

Merten did not join the miracle seekers. In the morning he decided that, as he expected his return to Fluentia to be a highly emotional experience, he did not want the whole fuss over a statue, weeping or not, to sidetrack him. Instead, he spent almost the whole of Good Friday reading in the garden. He even once more reread his Fonteluce notes. Repeatedly, he let his eyes roam the valley underneath the terrace, thus moving mentally towards the city of which – apart from a castle associated with its history, but hidden from sight unless he walked along the winding main road underneath him – there was no sign whatsoever. Long after nightfall, he still sat out there; and when the candles had burned down and he got up to retire, he felt he was in the right frame of mind for his Holy Saturday adventure.

Small wonder that, the day after, he arrived far too early for the festivities. Yet, Fluentia was already crowded – especially in the cathedral precinct, traditionally the scene of the day's main spectacle. As everybody else, Merten was eventually going to elbow his way through to vantage ground. But with time on his hands and led by curiosity, he walked straight past the temple of St. John the Baptist and round the nearest street corner, to see what had become of his onetime local and storehouse of Fluentia tales. There it still was – unmistakably still the haunt of little artisans and country folk rather than the elegant citizen or even tourists. He peeped through the open door and, as the place was not very busy, instantly caught the eye of the host. Before the man – who seemed not to have aged at all – could recognize him, Merten stepped back. He had long consigned the place to memory; and something told him that there he wanted it to remain.

He wandered about for a little while. Should he go to the café now – or wait until later? He did feel thirsty; but when he emerged into the square with the café, he decided to go to the place across from it. He sat down outside and ordered a mineral water. As he studied the building opposite, he was surprised at how anonymous it appeared to him. He closed his eyes and let the four frescoed ladies pass in review – but soon, they gave way to another image. Of course: here, in this other place outside which he was sitting, he had in the early stages of their relationship had meetings with the Fandango girl. Only a few decades before that, the bar had been the haunt of a group of famous men of letters from Fluentia and elsewhere, a fact which fascinated Silvana. For a moment, his mind went blank; then, silently, he repeated her name. No doubt she was married, with children. They had in fact written to each other after her departure, but then lost contact. Yet he was amazed, whenever he remembered her, how strong the recollection still was. There had been other women since – women of whom he mostly thought with gratitude. But, yes, the Fandango girl had been special.

Merten paid and got out of his chair. He knew he had better hurry if he wanted to make it back to the cathedral in time. There, intoned by the archbishop, the *Gloria in excelsis Deo* would in less than an hour fill the air above the expectant crowds. And then the rite which he had come to see would be celebrated – a rite the origin of which was a dramatic conflict between orient and occident: the medieval crusades. More precisely: the first of these and the taking of the Holy City by the crusaders.

So back to the cathedral he went. What people came here for on Holy Saturday was to watch a white dove carry a flame from some kind of triumphal chariot, positioned outside, into the cathedral and through the nave right up to the altar

– from where the bird was to return to the chariot. The dove of course was not a real dove but a contraption which, as he had been told or read somewhere, travelled along a steel cable and was therefore not prone to serious accidents. Originally the bird's flight was, according to how it went, seen as a good or a bad omen by the crowd. It was said that those spectators – a great many – who used to come in from the countryside near Fluentia, interpreted the event in terms of a forecast of the next harvest. What else? Whilst recapitulating what he knew, he had arrived. And what a great feeling it was: standing there, anonymously in the midst of a multitude, with Fluentia cathedral and its majestic bell tower on one and the ancient temple of St. John the Baptist on the other side!

He had not felt as good for years. His heart operation seemed long past – and already, more than once since his last night at Charlottenfels, he had played with the idea of taking up something bold and wild. Who knew, maybe something like motor car racing. He had always been unusually energetic and was, in spite of his slight build, rather strong. He also felt almost ageless – perhaps this was because for a long time his handicap had held him back while other people ran themselves down. Only about a month ago, when still not quite so well, he saw some fellows he had once gone to school with: inactive lumps, with no waist and not even a neck left between their head and shoulders. Merten remembered them as dreadful bullies. And yet, when he passed them in the local high street near his ancestral home, they suddenly seemed so small. Although largely indifferent after so many years, he had, to his surprise, felt pity rather than satisfaction.

With his mind once more gone astray, he failed to witness the arrival of the chariot. Traditionally, the chariot was drawn through the city by two pairs of oxen – the animals almost disappearing underneath sumptuous garlands – and accompanied by musicians and men in armour, and by the four historical football teams of Fluentia. As the religious service in the temple of St. John the Baptist was about to finish, Merten was at leisure to watch how it was decided by lot which team would take on which in their annual tournament in June. For this tournament, known as the most brutal amongst Fluentia's time-honoured rituals, all the players had to dress in historical costume – just as they did this very morning. And what a fine body of men each team was! However, the glances some players exchanged with their rivals were telling; no doubt the tournament, a pageant in the eyes of the public, was just as much an occasion for old scores to be settled. As the four teams represented the four old quarters of the city of Fluentia, the event was always more than only a game.

All of a sudden, everything seemed to be happening at once. Someone – a group rather, presumably of clerics – had arrived with the flints which for centuries already had been used to kindle the flame the dove was to carry. Reportedly, these stones were splinters from the Holy Sepulchre and had been brought here by a son of Fluentia: the very man who first raised the standard of the victorious crusaders on the walls of the Holy City. Like everyone around him, Merten stood on tiptoe – but such was the crush that, like most people, he did not even see the dove take off. There was the *Gloria in excelsis*, there was smoke, there were fireworks, there were the cathedral bells … and eventually the bells of all Fluentia started ringing, thus announcing the Feast of the Resurrection. There had also been shouts in between – and it was only later that he learnt how the dove had at some stage tilted and threatened to fall off. What an ill-fated omen this must have seemed to the superstitious among the onlookers! But everything was over in what he guessed were barely five minutes. And as the four oxen reappeared and were put to the chariot, and as the crowd began to empty into the thoroughfares of the city centre, he watched how hundreds of pigeons, scared away by the fireworks, returned to the cathedral and their abodes high up on some cornice or in the bell tower.

Looking about him and deliberating what to do next, he realized he wanted another drink – a strong drink this time. And this time, the café with the frescoes was the obvious choice. Slowly, he began to walk, still pondering over the ritual he had just – at least partly – witnessed. Originally, on the same day, the flints supposed to be splinters from the Holy Sepulchre had been used to light a big candle on the altar of Fluentia cathedral; from this candle the faithful would receive the sacred flame, which they would then carry to their own and their relatives' houses. Hence the people of Fluentia must have seen the man who brought the stones back with him from the first crusade as a kind of light-bearer. Strangely, this man's family originated from Fonteluce – *nomen est omen*! As this thought occurred to Merten, it also occurred to him that the same family had eventually been responsible for one of the darkest chapters in the history of Fluentia: it was they who, in a later century – and not far from his villa at Opaco – plotted an abortive attempt on the life of Fluentia's most magnificent prince. An attempt which took place inside the cathedral.

He had arrived in front of the café and, without a glance at the people sitting outside, walked straight through the open door. Sure enough: the place seemed virtually unchanged. Except for the staff, he thought, as he ordered a drink. Standing at the bar, he reacquainted himself with every detail within sight. There seemed to be two maids working in the kitchen now, but neither of them provided the sort of spectacle he had once been addicted to. However, when he looked up to the ceiling, he felt as if he were greeted by old friends. And when he walked over to the corner underneath the fourth fresco, there was no doubt: the lady in it, his at one time Dark Lady, had reddish hair. He emptied his drink, went back to the bar and ordered another. He thought the frescoes were in an astonishingly good condition; but as he now needed glasses to study detail, and had left his at Opaco, an in-depth examination of the four ladies would have to wait until a later visit. Again, from his observation post, Merten looked around him. And as he stood there, he was suddenly overpowered by the recollection of his recent interview at Opaco: of his encounter with the woman who had applied for the post of housekeeper. The shape of her thighs! It was the kind of sight that could in an instant undo every gentlemanly notion in him. In her leggings and with her very short hair, she looked like temptation in the guise of a medieval knight's page – her shape, however, bulgingly female. No mistaking of the gender, as in a famous bard's comedies. And no doubt every medieval knight would have dragged such a woman into the nearest bushes! He had not offered her the job – although there were no other candidates, he had told her he would decide after having seen all applicants. Of course he intended to give her an answer; but did he, he asked himself while sipping his Armagnac and once more looking up to the ceiling, really want to complicate his few months at Opaco?

★ ★ ★ ★ ★

I am glad I ended the story of the weeping madonna only provisionally. She is back in the village underneath the monastery! The triumph of mayor and district attorney – and of the scientists at Fluentia University, for that matter – was short-lived: the villager whom they were confident to unmask as a trickster has successfully refused to undergo blood tests. Admittedly, the statue has not wept again. But it seems that the faithful do not need any more tears; nearly three thousand of them came on Holy Saturday and gathered outside the parish church, watching in ecstasy as the madonna returned. And there she is now: in a niche, behind bulletproof glass. Of course the fellow who had set up a stall with replicas on the road is back in business — I can now even see him from my terraced garden, as he has had the cheek of moving farther down towards Opaco.

This morning, when I went for a stroll, I was actually tempted to go and look at his figures. But first, like almost every day since I arrived here, I walked over to the little church. There, I was distracted by the man who had first told me about the madonna: I bumped into the sacristan. As he is a knowledgeable man, I always chat to him — we have even agreed to meet for a game of chess one day. Yet, his attitude perplexes me; whenever — and however tactfully — I express some doubt about the "miracle," he changes the subject. Today he became agitated, though. He had walked back to the main road with me; and there, some people in a car asked us how far it was to the shrine of 'her who wept for mankind.' I did not even say a word, but maybe the sacristan disliked the expression on my face. 'Remember this is a venerated place!' he said to me, rather sternly. Then — perhaps I struck him as taken aback, or because he is almost twice my age — his manner, just as abruptly, became almost paternal. He told me how the village and the monastery high up on the hillside had ages ago become a centre of pilgrimage. A monk, who was dying, expressed a wish to see his sister one last time. This sister lived far away, in another country — but according to the sacristan an angel bore her to her brother's bedside. Henceforth the sister led a solitary life in a cave near the village, her only food being fruit and roots. Knights and holy matrons are said to have visited. When she herself died, more than eleven hundred years ago, the monastery was built and the wild places round it were cultivated.

★ ★ ★ ★ ★

Mankind seems to distress the madonna no longer: since her return she has not shed a single tear. And for some ten days, nothing worth mentioning has happened at Opaco. Hence, inevitably, I spend more time down in Fluentia.

There is something, though, which I feel I ought to commit to paper. It has to do with those dreams of mine when, after the Sirconi disaster, I became obsessed with the four frescoed ladies on the ceiling of the café. More precisely: what I am about to write down concerns the dream about the duchess who, according to her murderer, had died while washing her hair. Well, three days ago I drove to the airport to collect a weighty suitcase which, as I did not need its contents urgently, I had left there – and on my way back, some impulse prompted me to leave the motorway and take a country road to Greti. There, in the villa, I realized to my surprise that upon my first visit and subsequently in my dream I had got a detail wrong. The duchess was not, as popular belief has it, strangled in the first floor saloon with the vaulted ceiling: she ended her life in a corner chamber on the ground floor. Here her contemptuous husband, his victim no longer twisting in his hands, threw her corpse to the ground as if he was ridding himself of an unwanted dog. A piece of rope that hangs from the ceiling put me on the right track; 'it's only a symbol,' the custodian, whom I questioned, said – but he then told me what I have just written down.

★ ★ ★ ★ ★

Once more, Merten stood in the café and raised his eyes to the ceiling. Then, acting on impulse, he went over to the till and addressed the woman who sat behind it and who now seemed to be the boss. He told her that, a decade earlier, he used to be a regular guest – and that, like then, he still felt bewitched by the four frescoes. She laughed – he obviously was a man of taste, she said. The portraits, she then added, had been restored only recently. Merten nodded – had he not, on Holy Saturday, concluded that the frescoes were in a remarkably good condition?

The woman pointed to the one in the corner: 'Quite a few years ago, the restorer improved this one.'

An alarm bell started ringing in Merten's head. 'Improved?' he asked.

She hesitated, perhaps sensing that he was knowledgeable about art. Anyway, she then said: after the restorer had attended to the one fresco, she and her staff felt that the other three would benefit from his work as well.

'Doesn't the result meet with your approval?' she inquired. Merten, who was eager to hear more, hastened to reassure her.

'I am glad you think so,' she said with a smile. She shifted in her seat, revealing a pair of well-shaped legs, and he had to admit to himself that he found the whole woman rather attractive. 'Everybody here was pleased, and this is why I allowed him to put his signature underneath each fresco.' She thought, she added, that this was the least she could do for the man – 'especially when I found out that it was he who had already once, some twenty or thirty years before, restored the frescoes.'

Merten felt as if electrified. After paying her a compliment on the café in general and on maintaining high standards – he admitted he had years ago left Fluentia, but was now back for a while – he asked the woman to excuse him. Pointing to the ceiling, he confessed to being irresistibly drawn to the ladies depicted there.

'I can see this,' she said with a smile, at the same time brushing back a stray lock of blond hair with her hand – 'hence,

I hope we shall see you again here before long.' For more than one reason, Merten answered in the affirmative.

Once more, now with his glasses on, he stood right underneath the fresco in the corner. "Restored by W. Cesini," he read in small letters at the lower extremity of the portrait. He stepped across to look at the other three portraits – and found the same name again. All of a sudden, he became painfully aware of his recent operation. Cesini! The recollection had made his pulse rate almost double. Cesini was the unkempt fellow who, in his Strange Fruit days, had watched him study the frescoes – and who had once offered to work for him. So this Cesini was the man who had already restored the frescoes once previously – the restorer Merten had asked Pepalmar about! His thoughts returned to what the woman at the till had just said. When, he asked himself, had Cesini started "improving" the Samira picture? Just before he, Merten, realized that it again looked as it once did when he had started coming to the café? Or did the restorer have a hand in the gradual transformation which he believed he had witnessed? Merten decided that he definitely had to cultivate the acquaintance of the woman who was now the boss in the café.

★ ★ ★ ★ ★

I have had another lengthy talk with Gastone, the steward. Needless to say that I brought up the weeping madonna. His quick reply, given his silence on the subject so far, came as a surprise. Gastone dismisses the whole madonna thing as a hoax. 'There are,' he said, 'some sinister forces at work in this area – occult groups, you know.' I could not help laughing. But he was undeterred; noticeably shivering, he told me how rumours had it that in some places up in the hills dead bodies were, rather than being buried, boiled in cauldrons at night. 'Occult groups,' he reaffirmed, with a demonstrative nod of his head.

It was then that I remembered how, in the days I had briefly been Pepalmar's neighbour in the hills above Fonteluce, the wealthy young proprietor of a villa was found dead in his swimming pool. Reportedly, the pool was a sea of blood. According to the marshal, the young man – who had suffered terrible injuries – had been torn to pieces by his four dogs. Consequently, the animals were all put down. Pepalmar saw things differently. 'The marshal is not only an imbecile,' he said; 'the man is venal.' In fact, I remember our talk very well. 'This,' the professor added, 'was the work of Satanists.'

I must ring Pepalmar. I did, when at Charlottenfels, drop him a line with the news of my forthcoming return to Fluentia, but this was before I knew where I would stay. But I digress. Gastone, when we talked about the madonna, said that the owner of my villa had expressed a wish to make my acquaintance. I asked where the man lived. 'Not at Opaco'; 'but' – the steward pointed in the direction of the little church – 'he does own another house over there, where he sometimes stays.' Then, almost as if he were talking to himself, he added: 'Behind the church, at Alpiniano's Court.' I waited for more – but the steward would not be drawn. Instead, he mounted the steed one of his men had saddled for him. As he must have done in his youth, coming from an area famous for its horses and horsemen, Gastone rides every day.

★ ★ ★ ★ ★

More miracle news: the day after I had had my long chat with Gastone, the madonna wept in the presence of the mayor! The man – again, Gastone is my source - had finally condescended to take a look at the statue. He had even demanded that the priest remove the bulletproof glass, so that he could touch the figure behind – and when the priest handed him the statue, it started weeping. 'From that moment,' Gastone said, 'the mayor has been a convert.' The steward gave me a sardonic smile. 'So what do you make of this, sir?' He did not even wait for an answer – he believed, he said, that the mayor had simply woken up to the commercial potential of the madonna. The man had the mentality of a tourism operator. 'The trouble is, of course, that by supporting the miracle thesis he has pitched himself against his erstwhile – and always most unlikely – ally, the district attorney. But as that execrable marshal at Fonteluce is one of the mayor's henchmen, the district attorney is not exactly making much progress right now.'

The fact that the Fonteluce marshal has authority over Opaco was news to me. Anyway, I have definitely warmed to Gastone. In the way he observes age-old customs and responds to superstitions of a pagan nature, he is perhaps the classical local – but at the same time he can be amazingly sharp. Thus, it was he who told me that the abbot in the monastery above the village now favours a prosaic reading of the miracle. 'He too knows what is going on in the hills – and he must suspect that somebody, or some devilish group, is trying to undermine the church by having played a prank.' Small wonder the abbot, as Gastone tells me, intends to shortly exorcise the villager in whose garden the madonna had first wept blood.

★ ★ ★ ★ ★

'Leander, where on earth are you?' Pepalmar, although probably nearing eighty, sounded as youthful as ever.

Merten explained where he had found a place; adding that he had meant to telephone earlier, but that the first two weeks since his return had been most eventful.

The professor laughed – but then reminded him that, as a convalescent, he was supposed to take things easy. 'Who looks after you in that big house?' Pepalmar knew the villa at Opaco.

Merten admitted that so far he had been coping on his own, but that he was looking for a housekeeper. He realized he had almost forgotten about the woman who had applied for the job – and what a woman! Was he creating a problem for himself? He should have employed her immediately! His thoughts were cut short.

'I sat outside your favourite café the other day,' Pepalmar said – 'with somebody who knows you.' The professor added it was on Holy Saturday. His companion thought for a moment to have recognized Merten entering the place. She had suddenly gone quiet, and then pointed to the door. "*Wasn't that Leander?*" she asked. Pepalmar had dismissed the question as mere fantasy – he admitted that it was only days later when he received the letter in which Merten announced his return.

'It was me,' Merten said.

'How come, on Holy Saturday?'

As the woman who had offered her domestic services was still on Merten's mind, the question registered slowly. After a pause, he told Pepalmar he had always wanted to see the Holy Saturday ritual in front of Fluentia cathedral.

Later on the same day, Merten drove down to Fluentia since he wanted to buy some books. Afterwards, he decided it was time to pay his respects to the four frescoed ladies and also renew his acquaintance with the new boss who sat at the till underneath them. When he walked across the square towards the café, he passed a short-haired woman in black trousers. What a bottom! He turned round – and she turned round too. It was the woman who had come to see him at Opaco.

'Fancy meeting you here!' Merten said, trying to disguise his voyeuristic tendencies.

'Why not?' she answered, obviously amused. Her deep voice suddenly struck him. She pointed to the café: 'I worked over there, years ago – didn't you realize?'

He was thunderstruck. He had, because of her very short hair and the few grey streaks, not recognized her. Also, he had of course not been at leisure to study her curves when she presented herself at Opaco. But now, in an instant, he remembered how once he had spied on the kitchen-maid taking a bus to the hills north of Fluentia, where she obviously lived.

Strange Fruit! To his own surprise, he heard himself say that he had intended to call her – that he would like her to be his housekeeper.

She smiled. 'With pleasure, Dr. Merten.'

They agreed on the Monday after, and then she was gone. Merten, more than ever, needed a drink. But contrary to his first inclination, he went to the place across from the café. Having just employed Strange Fruit was quite enough for him – how could he possibly, at the same time, cope with the four frescoed ladies?

★ ★ ★ ★ ★

Her name was Amaranta. She had started work at the villa the week after their chance encounter, and only three days later Merten had to admit to himself that her presence made a great difference. Being, so to speak, privy to everything she did whilst there, he realized that her enormous sexual appeal and the energy she poured into the housework were evenly balanced. Besides, she was a fantastic cook. And to think that he had hesitated to employ her! Whatever powers were responsible for their meeting outside the café, he was most grateful to them. This, he said to himself, was what recuperation should be like. Yet, he had set himself some tasks. One of them was difficult – and although Amaranta seemed a possible source of information, he decided he would only tentatively broach the subject. But, as his subject was the Samira fresco, there was an alternative source: the new woman in the café. His other task seemed easier: he wanted to finally see the weeping madonna himself and get a clearer idea of what was going on in the village and the monastery high up on the hillside.

The Samira fresco was foremost on his mind when next he went down to Fluentia. It was on a Monday morning, and as most shops were closed, he reckoned that the café would be fairly quiet. As indeed it was – the woman at the till just sat there, leafing through some magazine or brochure. She recognized Merten instantly and expressed her pleasure at seeing him again. As the occasion was ideal, he came straight to the point. He told her he was an art historian – to which she replied he had struck her as scholarly. He pointed to the corner: he said he had always been especially interested in the fresco over there. Whereas the other three ladies were by the same painter, this one – which was better, he said with emphasis – was by someone different. But, he added, he had a few questions about it. He had studied the woman's face quite attentively all the while: what should he tell her next? Nothing, he decided, about the transformation of the picture he believed to have witnessed.

'Do you remember when the restorer started' – he paused, and then opted for her own terminology – 'started improving the fresco?'

She shook her head. 'There was never a schedule,' she said, 'not even when he restored the three others. He was quite free to come in whenever he pleased, be it on the day of closure or even late at night. In a way,' she went on, 'Cesini was part of "the family".' Merten indicated surprise. 'Well, he had been – or even was at the time, I don't know – married to the kitchen-maid.'

Wasn't it great, Merten thought: Cesini being the ex-husband of his housekeeper! The man who once – or maybe still

– screwed the surgeon's widow at Fonteluce. Well, he did not care for the surgeon's widow. But for this ungainly individual to have been married to Amaranta! It suddenly struck him that he had practically forgotten about her previous incarnation as Strange Fruit. Wasn't it interesting how a fetish stopped being a fetish, once you perceived the object of your fantasy as a real person?

'I can't really tell you more,' the woman at the till said, thus ending his ruminations – 'nobody here knows much about the frescoes anyhow.'

Merten, who had come to the same conclusion a decade earlier, told her not to worry. He then said he had returned to Fluentia not to work but to relax.

Her face lit up. In this case, she said, she hoped to have him amongst her invitees on the following Saturday. 'The café closes early, as we are celebrating its 150th anniversary – which means that we have a private reception here from 7 pm. You, as an art historian with such an interest in the place, would be a most welcome guest – may I count on your coming?'

He accepted happily. 'I am Leander Merten,' he added, with an apology for not having introduced himself before.

'Berenice Miolane,' she responded, holding out her hand.

Good God, he thought when he stood in the square outside: not only had Cesini been free to work on – or "improve" – the frescoes, he had even enjoyed the freedom of Amaranta's fabulous curves! For a while, Merten walked aimlessly through Fluentia. His housekeeper, he concluded, was probably the key to everything. But this was a delicate case; on the one hand, he now knew quite a few things about her private life – and on the other hand, he had always kept professional and private matters separate. The question was, of course, what sort of a relationship she had with Cesini right now. Anyway, as he was getting to know her better day by day, he was confident that he would at some stage hear what he was after – she was, although intelligent, not complicated.

So how did he want to spend the rest of this already eventful day? He contemplated ringing Pepalmar to ask whether the professor was free to meet. Or should he go back to Opaco and from there pay a visit to the weeping madonna? Ladies first, Merten thought – and soon he sat in his car and drove into the hills again.

★ ★ ★ ★ ★

I always knew that the statue was small – but as it has been talked about so much, I had no longer imagined it quite that small. Maybe she is about fifteen inches high. Anyway, the madonna did not weep whilst I looked at her. When I left the church – which was not easy, given the crowds still trying to get through the narrow door – I saw Gastone's horse outside the butcher's. The moment I crossed the little square, the steward emerged from the shop. He seemed quite amused when I told him why I had come up to the village. 'No tears,' I added instantly – as I have no doubt he realizes that I share his reservations. 'She has remained dry-eyed since I last spoke to you, sir,' he replied – adding with a chuckle that the traces of the blood the mayor beheld would very likely soon fade. He also told me that the exorcism the abbot conducted on the villager in whose garden the madonna had originally stood produced no results. 'No doubt the district attorney feels his moment has come – just look at these poker-faced fellows in their boring suits!' I did notice that the place was teeming with people whose looks answered Gastone's description. 'Well,' the steward said, 'as the marshal is an obstacle, the district attorney has called in the bureau of criminal investigation.'

And all this because of what some people believed they had seen on the tiny face of a statue! I suddenly remembered how, in my early student days, I had visited a great Gothic cathedral some two and a half hours south of Fluentia. This cathedral had been built to commemorate a similar event. In a nearby village, the host had started bleeding during communion. The event was later immortalised in a painting by one of the country's greatest artists. And it was this same event which, more than seven hundred years ago, had prompted a then Father of the Church to establish the Feast of Corpus Domini. Even this miracle, I believe, some scientists have recently managed to – or at least tried to – explain. It might be an idea to research their findings. Wouldn't it be quite a feat for the present occupant of the villa at Opaco to add to the confusion surrounding the madonna!

★ ★ ★ ★ ★

'I hear you have had a look at the miraculous statue,' Amaranta said.

Merten – it was the day after, and he had just sat down for lunch – could not help saying he was surprised that she knew.

His housekeeper laughed. 'This is a small place – and in this country, news travels fast anyway!' She gave him a questioning glance. 'Don't forget you are here to recuperate, Dr. Merten.' He waited for what was to come. 'I hope you are not taking this whole affair too seriously,' she then said. She hesitated. 'I know one of the people who make money out of it.' Merten smiled encouragingly. 'My ex-husband,' she finally said. He was stunned. 'No doubt you have seen the man who sells replicas of the madonna?' Merten said he had – but only from his terrace, not face to face. 'Well – that's him.' He felt even more stunned: Cesini selling statues underneath his villa at Opaco!

She hesitated again. 'His name is Walter Cesini – I don't know whether you remember: he once, perhaps fifteen years ago, asked you for work.'

He admitted that he did remember. Her confidentiality had disarmed him. She stood in front of him, frank and – as always – very sexual. What a woman, he thought. She would be anyone's perfect accomplice; he had to find out whether she was completely finished with Cesini or perhaps felt she had to somehow shield him.

The weekend was approaching, and as he had this invitation to the party in the café, he thought he had better meet Pepalmar before. When he telephoned his old friend, the professor insisted that he come and see where he and his wife were now living. Once again, Merten was aware of time passing. Although he had met Pepalmar's wife on at least two of his brief Fluentia visits, she was still the new wife to him – which was how her husband had labelled her, in his at the time incessant references to her.

Their place was really out in the sticks – much more so than his villa at Opaco. But as the Pepalmars had only recently moved from Fonteluce, it was the ancient little town they all soon talked about. Merten had decided beforehand that he would not yet tell the professor who his housekeeper was. Nevertheless, he did hope to hear one or two things in connection with her.

'What about that surgeon's widow – the one who had a fling with her handyman,' he finally asked – 'no doubt it was she who spotted me recently, when you sat outside the café?'

'It actually wasn't,' Betty, Pepalmar's wife, answered.

'No, it was a friend from the university,' Pepalmar said quickly – we will invite you with her one day.' Merten's mind was elsewhere – but the professor had guessed. 'The surgeon's widow left,' he said; 'she had become quite a laughing stock, especially as her handy ... or rather fancy man set up house with his ex-wife again. This last bit,' Pepalmar said, turning to Betty, 'is bad news for Leander; he once rather admired that ex-wife's ...' – he checked himself, but could not suppress his musical laugh – '... generous proportions.' Merten always knew he loved the man. As often when he had one of his fits of mirth, Pepalmar instantly turned serious again. 'I am told that she kicked him out soon after. I don't know the man at all, but apparently he had long been involved in some shady activities – and finally, she found out.'

After Betty had served some ham and melon, it seemed inevitable to Merten to mention the weeping madonna.

'Total rubbish!' the professor said – 'but no doubt you have already come to this conclusion.' Merten waited for the rest. 'Perhaps somebody painted the face of the statue with a substance that liquefies when the temperature rises – or when the statue is moved.' There was a pause. 'You know' – Pepalmar was dead serious – 'I have often thought of that Sirconi sale; and I have come to the conclusion that your verdict was probably correct.' He put his hand on the younger man's arm: 'Leander, as you are at leisure right now, I would love you to contribute to the madonna debate.'

Although momentarily dazed by the reference – and tribute – to his involvement in the ill-fated Fluentia auction of the century, Merten laughed. 'I am an art historian – I am not an expert on miracles!'

'Yes; but you also have a detective's instinct, and this is probably what's needed.' Merten, who knew he was positively hooked on the whole madonna business, remained silent. 'Keep an eye on the mayor and the marshal, though,' Pepalmar added – 'these two are up to anything, if they smell a profit or advancement. And no doubt somebody up there, maybe even a group from outside, is in league with them.'

★ ★ ★ ★ ★

On Saturday, he was too early for the party. As there was not enough time to do something else, he went to the place opposite the café and sat down at one of the tables outside. While he sipped his drink, his thoughts returned to the afternoon at Pepalmar's – and from there a long way down memory lane. He should, he said to himself, ask the professor whether he knew what had become of the Fandango girl. La Fandango, as Pepalmar used to call her. Not only had Pepalmar still taught when she attended Fluentia University: it had always puzzled Merten how the professor seemed to attract letters from long gone students. Or how he just knew about them. So when had Pepalmar last heard anything relating to Silvana? No doubt married, with kids, Merten thought. He remembered her eyes: almond-shaped, with sometimes – it rather added to her elegance – a slightly roguish expression. Who again, in ancient Fluentia, was the poet who had listed such traits as paramount when commenting on female beauty?

When, half an hour later, he rose to join the people he had seen enter the café, he wondered whether any of the faces would be known to him. No doubt, Berenice had selected her guests from amongst the affluent Fluentia crowd. But whoever the guests: his main objective was getting further acquainted with the hostess. As he hardly ever, when meeting women, took note of wedding rings, he had no idea about her personal circumstances. Yet, if asked he would have said that Berenice was probably unattached.

She wore a close-fitting trouser dress and against its colour – a pale green – her mane of blond hair looked splendid. The waiter who stood guard at the entrance seemed to have expected Merten, and Berenice had even taken his arm as he entered – but then there was some scuffle outside, probably caused by people who did not know of the private function, and she rushed back to the door. Merten was soon engaged in conversation with various guests. Somehow to his relief, there was no one he knew from his earlier Fluentia days.

Inevitably, he felt drawn towards the Samira fresco – and when everybody made a rush for a new round of canapés that was being served, he went over to the corner underneath. As he looked up to the ceiling, it seemed impossible to him that he had ever believed to see the woman portrayed there as the buxom kitchen-maid – who now, surprisingly, was his housekeeper! Yet, he knew that the picture's metamorphosis had not been a product of his imagination. But where was the proof? And what exactly had been the reason or purpose behind the changes? His eyes wandered over the picture: from the courtesan to the putti who, tumbling on the floor and flying through the air, surrounded her. Again, he thought that the work was a good one – and he had to admit to himself that Cesini, when last restoring both it and the other frescoes, had done an excellent job.

'May I ask if you are here in a professional capacity, Dr. Merten?'

The voice belonged to a man – he was casually, but expensively dressed and seemed to be in his mid-sixties – who had obviously watched him study the fresco. Merten had not noticed his approach and had no idea who he was.

'Dupré,' his vis-à-vis introduced himself – adding, clearly amused that Merten was none the wiser, that he was the owner of the villa at Opaco.

'What a surprise!' – Merten, with an apology for not knowing his landlord's name, shook hands.

Dupré admitted that, likewise, he had been ignorant of his tenant's identity — but that Gastone had enlightened him a few days ago. He then pointed in the direction of Berenice. 'Our hostess is of course delighted to have a foreign art historian here; hence I was told of your presence the moment I entered.'

After a brief glance at the frescoed ceiling, Dupré looked straight at Merten again. 'I may as well tell you that I have always admired your knowledge and judgement.'

Merten, who could not think of any previous link between them, was perplexed — 'How come?' he finally asked, as the man seemed to expect a reaction.

'Well, I was aware of your involvement in the Sirconi sale — at the time, I mean.' This conversation promised to be worthwhile, Merten thought. 'Your assessment of the statue was correct,' Dupré continued; 'in fact, you alone got all the details right.'

Given that the vendor had remained anonymous, Dupré's declaration was intriguing.

'May I ask how you know?' Merten ventured.

His interlocutor explained that he was acquainted with the vendor — and had of course also seen the figure.

'Has he meanwhile sold it privately?'

This time, Merten got a vague answer. Without saying yes or no, Dupré finally remarked that the present owner of the statue spent much of his time abroad — 'and as he has no family, one rarely knows where he is or what he is doing.'

They were interrupted by Berenice. 'You don't seem to have time to talk to me, Leander,' she teasingly said, again linking arms with him. Merten was amused and at the same time rather pleased with her familiarity.

'It is all my fault,' Dupré said – 'we not only have the same interests, we are even neighbours.' Berenice looked questioningly from the one to the other – and then at the older man again. But Dupré was unwilling to enlarge. Announcing that he had to go, he kissed Berenice's hand. 'It would be a pleasure to see you at my house for an apéritif, Dr. Merten,' he said, turning around.

'It is my pleasure to accept,' Merten replied. 'Gastone has already said that the owner of the villa would want to see me. But he did not tell me your name.'

Dupré laughed. 'Gastone is quite a free spirit, you know.'

Merten said he had already come to the same conclusion. 'However, he did show me where I would find you.' Dupré nodded approvingly. 'At Alpiniano's Court,' Merten added, remembering Gastone's aside. For a moment, Dupré looked strangely disconcerted. But then, taking leave, he was his engaging self again; he told Merten how much he enjoyed their meeting, and that he would indeed telephone him as soon as he was at Opaco for a couple of days.

★ ★ ★ ★ ★

The morning after, at Opaco, Merten had a splitting headache. He had drunk far too much at Berenice's – quite consciously of course, he had to admit to himself. When more people had started to go and he too bade farewell to the hostess, she begged him to stay behind – she lived above the café, she said, and would value his opinion on a painting she had recently bought. He knew that he was walking into a trap, but the idea rather appealed to him; after all, it was months since he had last been with a woman, and Berenice was quite spectacular. To be fair to her: the picture she had bought – on impulse – needed, and deserved, to be examined by someone with a trained eye. But when he wanted to take it off the wall she said that she liked it, which was the most important thing, and that he could always come back another time and 'be really scholarly.' She laughed: 'Your dedication to your subject makes you irresistible, Leander! You must have driven countless women to despair.' She instantly became quite amorous, and he instantly began to drink more. He wanted to take her clothes off, but his recent operation worried him.

Finally, the clothes had come off. On the road to Opaco, the morning after, he remembered the look on her face after she had seen the scar on his chest. He knew that she had understood instantly – that she was a woman who had lived and who therefore had no need of an explanation, contrary to the prim and proper 'don't touch me' type he had never liked. He also remembered that some rather extensive lovemaking had followed – although he had no idea of when she ultimately switched off the lights or how long he had been asleep.

When Amaranta served his lunch, she lingered before going home, as she always did, for a couple of hours. 'You don't seem to be very well today, Dr. Merten – are you really taking things easy?'

He laughed. 'Yes. But I have decided that I need to do regular exercises again.' She looked amused, which for a moment quite unsettled him. 'What I mean,' he added, 'is that I want to build up stamina – so I shall buy myself a bicycle today. I intend to start going for rides into the hills.'

She still looked amused. 'I hadn't thought a bicycle was your kind of thing – given your style. But it seems a good idea.'

He decided that the moment to sound her on the restoration of the frescoes had come. 'I was invited to a reception down in Fluentia last night', he said – 'it was at your former place of work, the café. And guess whom I met there? Mr. Dupré, the owner of this villa.' She was visibly surprised with the last piece of information. 'An interesting man,' Merten added.

'Can you remember the first time you spoke to me?' he said after a pause. 'It was the only time you ever did speak to me, all those years ago when I frequented the café.' Deliberately, he gave her a reproachful look. She laughed – and as always when she allowed her softer side to show, she instantly looked younger. He felt that she was, whatever the reason, at present not spoilt with compliments.

'Was this when you asked my father about the frescoes?'

'Yes.' The fact that she remembered so easily made him wonder whether, at the time, she had known something about him and his activities. 'Why did you – or your father, for that matter – not tell me that your ex-husband had done the previous restoration of the frescoes?'

'I didn't know then – Cesini only told me when, a couple of years ago, he restored the frescoes again. And as for my father: he never wanted to have anything to do with or even know about Cesini. Hence, I cannot tell you whether he was aware that my ex had been the restorer.'

Again, in her reply, she struck him as absolutely frank – the only person out here, he thought, whom I can trust implicitly.

'How is your father, by the way?'

'He is dead.'

Merten, who remembered the old man's courtesy, said he was sorry to hear the news.

'He died four years ago.' Amaranta paused. 'Shortly after, Cesini and I were back together again – for a while.' She hesitated. 'I just needed a man in the house, Dr. Merten.' He indicated that he understood. She looked at him searchingly. 'Was it Dupré who told you that Cesini had restored the frescoes?'

'No. It was Berenice Miolane, a couple of weeks ago. She also tells me that Dupré is an avid and eclectic collector of artworks.' Then, with an afterthought, he said he was unaware whether Dupré knew much about the frescoes and their restoration.

'He does,' Amaranta said. Once more, she gave him that frank and knowing glance. 'May I say that I would not recommend close contact with Mr. Dupré to you?' Another pause. 'If it were not for him, I might still be with Cesini – although I am glad I am not.' She seemed lost in thoughts. 'Whatever Cesini's faults,' she then said, 'he did once show much early promise. This was when, as a youngster, he briefly attended art school.'

Merten, mindful of the quality of Cesini's latest job in the café, had no doubt that the man was talented. He decided to let the matter rest for a while.

'Why don't you sit down and eat with me, Amaranta? There is enough for both of us.'

'I can't,' she said – 'but thank you.' He waited, as he knew that she would explain. 'I have a retarded child at home, and the neighbours who used to look after him when I worked have left.'

'Did Cesini not take an interest in the boy?' Merten asked.

'He never did. The boy is not by him, anyhow.' She straightened herself up and he remembered the moment when he had first seen her in the kitchen of the café – which had made him liken the men around her to animals in the circus arena. 'He isn't really by anyone, if you like.' She laughed, but

87

this time it was a joyless laugh. 'I had a rather wild time when things first started to go wrong in my marriage. Shortly after, the boy was born.'

Merten recalled what Pepalmar had told him years ago. 'What is wrong with your boy?' he wanted to know.

'He just doesn't seem to grow up – and I never had the money to take him to the specialists the local doctor suggested.'

Merten nodded. 'I perfectly understand,' he said, 'that you cannot eat with me, but maybe you would allow me to come and see you and your son at some stage?' He had never imagined that she could look so embarrassed. 'On my bicycle, of course,' he added. She instantly laughed again, and again she appeared rejuvenated. 'But wait,' he said, 'I have a better idea. Why don't you just bring your boy with you one morning?'

★ ★ ★ ★ ★

Amaranta tells me that the madonna has wept blood again. Apparently, an elderly local woman who just happened to be praying in the church had first seen it. Visitors heard her shout ecstatically: 'Look, look: there is blood everywhere – Holy Mother of Christ, it is true!' The woman, who fainted, had to be resuscitated by the Fluentia ambulance team that is now permanently stationed in the village. Amaranta, who later on the same day did some shopping for me up there, went to the church herself. 'Indeed, Dr. Merten,' she said, 'there was blood everywhere. Or what looked like blood. Not only the statue's face, but even its gown was soaked in red liquid.' Then she gave me one of her peculiar and at the same time disarming looks. 'I am sure Cesini is doing well out of this. And' – she paused – 'maybe Dupré too.'

I am beginning to wonder about my housekeeper. There is no guile in what she says – but what else does she know? No doubt, it will eventually be forthcoming. The woman fascinates me. As she did all those years ago. What would she make of my, at the time, Strange Fruit obsession? I have certainly freed myself from it. Have I, really? She looks ravishing – and I cannot help noticing her glorious posterior, which she does have a tendency to exhibit. Luckily, I have all my life kept matters private and professional apart. To be precise: ever since, when barely twenty and sorting out my father's estate at Charlottenfels, I stupidly – because I was flattered – succumbed to the advances of an older woman.

★ ★ ★ ★ ★

It was three weeks after the party at the café. Merten, back from another night at Berenice's, walked through his garden and up the steps to the villa. No doubt his housekeeper had seen his car come up the road, since she waited for him in the entrance.

He noticed that her hair was becoming longer. Yes, he thought: if she had come for her interview the way she looked today, he would have recognized her. Strange Fruit! Looking back, it still seemed unbelievable to him that the object of his at one time obsession was now in his domestic service.

'Mr. Dupré has telephoned,' Amaranta said without ceremony. Although she regularly enquired about his health, she was never prying – not even when it was obvious, like now, that he had stayed elsewhere overnight. 'Dupré is at Opaco,' she added – 'he rang to invite you over to his place for an apéritif.'

Merten consulted his watch.

'Oh, you have plenty of time before lunch!' She smiled. 'My son has come with me today, and I am therefore a bit behind with my work – I haven't started in the kitchen yet.'

'Excellent,' Merten said; 'I was beginning to think you would never bring him here.' They had, as they talked, entered the house. Merten looked around. 'But where is he, your boy?'

'At the bottom of the garden. He thinks the place is wonderful. He is actually cutting back some of those late-flowering shrubs which you said had to be seen to.'

Merten was surprised. 'What's his name?'

Amaranta hesitated. 'Davide – like my paternal grandfather's. I always adored the name.'

Merten said it was a fine name. He then asked whether there was enough food in the house for her to prepare a meal for all three of them. Just as the first time when he had expressed an interest in her son, Amaranta looked embarrassed – but he detected that she was also pleased. As he said nothing else, she finally answered in the affirmative.

He told her he was going to telephone Dupré in order to see him – 'just say when you want me to be back.'

'In two hours?' she suggested.

'Perfect,' he said. And before he left to pay a visit to his landlord, he also told her that after lunch she was free to take the rest of the day off.

★ ★ ★ ★ ★

When he rang the bell, it struck him as odd that so far he had not taken much note of Dupré's house. It was right behind the little church, the apse of which was facing the road – in fact, the two buildings shared part of a wall. But the house was also tucked in underneath a cluster of huge old trees, and since the shutters of the only two windows which gave onto the approach were always closed, the place had simply not caught his fancy. Besides, the shady grove which served as a forecourt both to the entrance of the church and to the house was supposed to be the ancient site of Alpiniano's Court. Merten, who was intrigued by what seemed a riddle no one could or was willing to explain, had on various occasions studied the layout – once or twice even in the presence of the sacristan. As to former buildings or even a castle, fragments of a wall provided the only visible archaeological evidence; and some earthen mounds were suggestive of a defensive structure.

The interior of Dupré's house was surprisingly bare. Berenice had more than once told Merten that the man was a manic buyer of artworks, but there was no sign of any costly acquisitions here.

The host seemed to guess his visitor's thoughts. 'I keep most of my treasured possessions elsewhere,' he said with a sweeping gesture. 'Anyway: to your health, Dr. Merten!' Dupré raised his glass. 'Tell me: I saw you examine those frescoes in the café. What exactly do you make of them?' The man's eyes seemed to have narrowed.

Merten gave an evasive answer. After entering, he had twice broached the subject of the weeping madonna – the obvious reason being that, whatever one believed, it was the topic of local interest. Each time, Dupré had pretended not to hear and passed on to something else. Hence Merten did likewise when his host attempted to make him enlarge on the frescoes. His thoughts returned to the weeping madonna and to what Amaranta had said about Dupré. Afterwards, their conversation remained strangely inconclusive – small wonder, Merten thought on his way back to the villa, that in the end he even forgot to ask what his landlord knew about Alpiniano's Court.

★ ★ ★ ★ ★

Before entering the villa, Merten went down to the bottom of the garden. Davide was still there. What a big young fellow! When Merten greeted him, his hand almost disappeared into the boy's. The person to call upon when some opposition needs to be sorted out, he thought. He was also, in spite of their very brief exchange, struck by Davide's courtesy. It reminded him of Amaranta's late father - although Davide was almost twice the old waiter's size. There was not much wrong with the boy, Merten concluded.

Afterwards, at lunch, he realized that Davide was not good with words. But his guess was that the boy was probably autistic, and that the teachers had simply not bothered much. He also had a very slight limp, which Merten was sure could be corrected. Such things just happen to those who in their environment are underdogs, he thought – you are told that you are odd and then one day you begin to behave, or move, oddly. Merten decided to talk to the mother when he knew her son better. He made it clear straightaway that he wanted to see more of him: Davide had done commendable work in the garden, and Merten offered to pay him if he continued and came once or twice a week.

To his surprise, Amaranta had changed for lunch. Maybe she kept some clothes in the utility room he never entered, and which therefore was very much her own domain. She looked unusual but, as always, very good. Towards the end of the meal, her son got fidgety. Finally, he asked if he could go down to the garden again.

'Your Davide strikes me as a workaholic,' Merten said after the boy had gone.

The mother was very amused. 'He has never struck me that way. But then nobody has ever offered him a job, or anything, Dr. Merten. So this is a first!'

'You too have scored a first,' he said – 'I have never before seen you wear a skirt.'

She blushed. Would he ever, in his early spell as a regular of the café, have considered this possible: Strange Fruit blushing!

'Well, Dr. Merten,' she said, 'it's very simple: if you prefer a female employee to wear skirts, I shall henceforth comply.'

'No!' His answer was completely unpremeditated. 'You always look fabulous!'

She blushed again. Good God, he thought: where is this conversation leading to? He needed a change of subject – and it was readily at hand.

'I agree with your reservations about Dupré,' he said as she, still looking a bit uncertain, started clearing the table. She stood still and gave him a questioning look. He told her how buttoned up and at the same time artful Dupré had appeared to be when they met.

'That's him – precisely,' was her dry comment.

'He wanted to hear my view about the frescoes in the café,' Merten said. His housekeeper straightened herself up and waited. 'Tell me, Amaranta: shortly before I left Fluentia, more than ten years ago, one of these frescoes started looking different – had any staff member at the café noticed?'

She laughed. 'You must understand, Dr. Merten ...'

'Could you please call me Leander?' Again, he had said something which she had clearly not expected. 'After all,' he added with a smile, 'we are the same generation.'

'Are you sure?' The softener worked – she was laughing again.

'Very sure!' Day after day, he had had ample occasion to watch her. She could not be more than one or two years older than he; perhaps it was even the other way round.

'Well then ... Leander,' she resumed her thought, 'you must understand that none of us working at the café paid much attention to the frescoed ceiling. At least not on a regular basis. However, the answer to your question is yes. Both the barman and a young waiter eventually noticed.'

'And who changed the fresco?'

'Cesini did.'

There we are, Merten thought. 'When? And at whose request?' he asked.

'At nobody's.' She paused. 'Although our marriage was in tatters, Cesini had become quite crazy about me again. And as one evening each week I worked longer – I cleaned the place – he would sometimes come in, hang around, and accompany me home afterwards. And that's when he did it.'

'Did what?' Merten asked. The thought that Strange Fruit was at the time in need of an escort hit him painfully.

'Touch up the fresco. That's what he said it needed: being touched up. And as I knew that he is an able restorer, I saw nothing wrong with what he did.' Merten agreed. Amaranta seemed to search her memory. 'But he didn't tell me then that he had once before restored the frescoes,' she said slowly. 'He only admitted to it when Berenice Miolane asked him to do the whole lot.'

'Did anyone notice that the fresco suddenly resembled you?' he wanted to know after a while.

'Yes, the barman – and in the end even I did.'

'And what explanation did Cesini have to offer?' She was more embarrassed than ever. 'I can't possibly tell you, Dr. Merten – Leander,' she corrected herself. He waited. 'Cesini,' she said hesitatingly, 'told me one day that he hoped to have played a trick on you. On various occasions when he came to the café, he had seen you study the frescoes. I knew – again, Cesini had been the source – of your involvement in the Sirconi sale. He said that in front of a work of art, you had the better instinct than anyone in Fluentia; actually, he called you the man with the infallible eye.' Again she paused. 'Once, just before he started to work on the fresco, I overheard a telephone conversation of his with Dupré. He said he was afraid that you would find out. But what, I do not know.'

Merten decided that he had learnt enough – and that one day, whatever it was she felt she could not possibly tell him, he would hear more.

★ ★ ★ ★ ★

Later in the week, Merten telephoned Pepalmar. 'I shall be in Fluentia tomorrow,' he announced – 'and I believe you said that this is the day when you, once a week, go there.'

'Indeed,' the professor replied; 'so let's meet. As I won't be too busy, I can see you at any time.'

Merten suggested mid-morning at the café. Berenice had gone to visit some relatives in a seaside town; otherwise – she had started behaving rather possessively when they last met – he would have chosen another venue.

'The café is fine with me,' Pepalmar said. He added he would ask his university friend if she had time to join them. 'The lady who spotted you there on Holy Saturday, Leander.' Merten, in whose mind the mere thought of the café unloaded an abundance of female images, asked himself if he really wanted to meet any more women there. Pepalmar broke the momentary silence with a laugh. 'My bringing you and this lady together is supposed to be a treat for you – so please do show a touch of enthusiasm!'

His friend could not come, Pepalmar told him when the day after they met and sat down at one of the tables outside the café: it just so happened that, this week, she was showing a group of visitors from foreign universities around Fluentia.

'By the way: what about the Countess?' the professor wanted to know. 'You used to be rather good friends. Are you seeing her again?'

'Sadly, I am not,' Merten replied; 'that chain-smoking, video-addicted relative still lives with her, and I do not want to waste my time having to talk to him.'

Pepalmar nodded. 'Who would?' he said. He then asked about the weeping madonna, and Merten told him the latest episode with the elderly woman who had fainted. 'The whole thing is a hoax!' Pepalmar exclaimed – 'but maybe you already have a more analytical view to offer?'

Merten said he had not. He admitted that he shared Pepalmar's opinion, and also that he believed he knew one or two of the people who were somehow involved. 'Probably not all of them – but, yes, one or two. And these I do not know well enough.' He intended to say more, to tell his friend about his housekeeper and what he had learnt from her regarding Cesini; but the professor's mind seemed to have wandered off suddenly.

'Do you remember, Leander, how you once came to Fonteluce and' – Pepalmar looked towards the entrance of the café – 'asked me about the fresco, the good one, in there?'

'Certainly.' Merten, who had never told the professor of the transformation he believed to have witnessed, wondered what was coming.

'Well, I have seen its double.'

'What on earth do you mean?' Merten thought he had not heard properly.

When the professor realized the impact his words were having, he became more specific. 'I have seen an identical picture. Only: it is better than the one in there.'

This promised to be a memorable meeting, Merten thought. He called one of the waiters over to their table and ordered another drink for both of them.

'I didn't know that the fresco was of such importance to you,' the professor said. He smiled. 'You may need yet another drink.'

Merten, guided by a sixth sense, said he had little doubt. 'So where did you chance upon this identical picture?'

The professor laughed and squeezed the younger man's arm affectionately. 'Well – maybe I should first say that your accounts of your childhood and adolescence had always impressed me, back in those days when we were neighbours at Fonteluce.' He paused. 'Do you remember telling me about a certain château near to where your mother grew up? The nobleman who lived there, banished from the court for writing an amorous history of its protagonists, had decorated his bedroom walls with portraits of the great ladies of his age – some his real, some his imaginary lovers.' Pepalmar was in his element now. Merten felt he knew what was in store for him; but at the same time, he rejected the idea. 'Betty and I visited the château last year,' the professor said – 'the picture is there, on the ceiling of the bedroom.'

'Impossible,' Merten said. He remembered the pictures in the disgraced count's bedroom very well – in fact, they had probably been the early impulse to his career. Whenever, as a schoolboy, he spent his summer holidays in the small town where his mother had grown up, he visited the château and abandoned himself to the perusal of the portraits of those ladies. But Pepalmar's face told him that something else was to come.

'When were you last there, Leander?'

Merten, who paid a woman in the town to look after his mother's house, suddenly felt it was ages since he had last visited – seven, maybe eight years ago? And the professor's question made him realize that he had not set foot in the nearby château for about twenty years.

Pepalmar seemed to have guessed his thoughts. 'You will of course,' he continued, 'remember when the state acquired the château. But you probably don't know that in more recent years the state, on a couple of occasions, bought a picture to add to the collection.' The guess was right: Merten did not know. 'The picture I am talking about,' Pepalmar said, 'is one of these acquisitions. It is called *A Fluentia Beauty – believed to have been a courtesan.*'

After he had said goodbye to Pepalmar, Merten went straight to a travel agent's. Cesini, Dupré – whoever: the bastards! There was little doubt in his mind as to where from *A Fluentia Beauty – believed to have been a courtesan* had found its way into another country and why, there, it now graced a provincial collection. But he had no proof. And, of course, he wanted to see the picture. He was confident that a talk with the administrator of the château would supply him with at least some clues. He booked a flight to the airport that was nearest to his mother's town; and as Brionnac was a sleepy little place with no shops left, he also made arrangements with a car hire service.

On his way back into the hills he realized that the air at Opaco and not least his housekeeper had over the weeks contributed greatly to his recovery. Although Pepalmar's revelation and his impending journey made every fibre in his body tingle, he felt he was ready for a big challenge. Wasn't it amazing that Pepalmar should provide an instrumental clue to what was maybe the greatest puzzle he had ever been exposed to – and that the answer seemed to be waiting for him, so to speak, in his own backyard? Merten, on the road to Opaco, felt very elated. In his mind, he went over his talk with

Pepalmar again. When from far below he caught a glimpse of his villa, he remembered the last part of their exchange. Strange, he thought: that, given the circumstances, he had not forgotten to ask the professor about the Fandango girl. 'Ah, La Fandango,' the professor had exclaimed – 'how much more exciting than pictures! I believe I have some news of Silvana,' Pepalmar added slowly, 'but this can wait until we meet again. Your interest in the fresco and its twin is most intriguing, dear Leander, and I do not want to distract a man on a mission.' Merten, for the first time in the many years they had known each other, secretly cursed his friend.

Before he reached the last bend underneath the villa, he suddenly decided that it was time to reacquaint himself with Cesini. He slowed down quite abruptly, as the stall with the replicas of the madonna was positioned immediately after the bend and he wanted to give the impression that his interest was almost casual. There were no other people around. Cesini, who was rearranging his display, only looked up when Merten stood right in front of him and picked up a statue. The stallholder's face fell – but he instantly collected himself. Yet, it was obvious he did not know whether he should acknowledge that they had previously met. The natural actor in Merten took over. 'Long time no see' – and before Cesini could say something, Merten asked how much the replica cost. The stallholder seemed to take the question as a joke; but when it was repeated, he mentioned his price. 'Done!' Merten, who felt that his perception would henceforth benefit from being constantly exposed to a specimen of Cesini's work – albeit not the best – took a couple of banknotes out of his wallet. He was at leisure to study Cesini while the man looked for the right change. He appeared less neglected than on the few occasions they had met before – a time, as Merten now knew, when the restorer's marriage was breaking up. Short but with a broad chest, Cesini – who was about twenty years older than Merten – still looked very strong. And however furtive, on occasions, his glance could be: he had to be credited with a rather well-shaped head.

When Merten carried the statue to his car, Gastone appeared on foot from the direction of the little church. The steward made no effort at hiding his surprise.

'You, sir – buying one of those ridiculous figures?'

Merten smiled. 'I like this place,' he said; 'and I wanted something to remind me of it. Don't you think this is a rather meaningful souvenir?' He gave Gastone an eloquent look.

The steward, whatever he thought, took the comment as a cue. 'There is nothing happening up there,' he said, indicating with a gesture the distant village underneath the monastery. 'Maybe' – he chuckled – 'those grey-suited fellows from the bureau of investigation have given the madonna a fright.' There was however a surprise in store for those fellows, he added. 'You must go up there tomorrow evening, sir, and see how village people celebrate the event.'

'What event?' Although Amaranta had pointed out the highlights of the local calendar to him, Merten, his impending journey on his mind, had lost track.

'The night of St. John the Baptist is at hand, sir.' Gastone laughed. 'The celebrations will give the slick investigators from the capital a taste of what people up here believe in – and of how removed their beliefs are from scientific methods. Mind you' – the steward paused – 'the rascally marshal isn't making things easy for the chaps from the bureau.'

There was a moment's silence between them, as Merten had opened the booth to put the statue in his car.

'Have you ever met him, sir – the marshal?'

'I have. It is my ambition to kick the man.'

'Please let me know when you are ready,' Gastone said with a laugh; 'I would like to participate.'

Another one to trust, Merten thought. He had seen Amaranta go down to the garden of the villa, and as it was near the time when she normally finished her work, he pointed across to the semi-circle of farmhouses – did the steward want a lift? As he expected, Gastone declined; 'I'll be there before you, sir,' he said and started walking.

In his car, Merten realized that he had not seen the sacristan for what seemed like ages. When, just underneath the villa and the buildings which shielded it, he caught up with the steward, he pulled down his window.

'The sacristan?' Gastone shrugged his shoulders. 'The man isn't here all the time, you know. I have no idea what the arrangement is – but he travels quite often. Besides, he is also responsible for the church up there, the one with the madonna, as of course you know.'

'Good heavens! No, I did not know!' Merten exclaimed. 'How strange!' He paused, quite stunned. 'So where does the man live?' Merten had always assumed that the sacristan inhabited one of the few houses which, being scattered along the main road, he saw as part of Opaco.

'At Alpiniano's Court,' the steward said.

'You mean: at Mr. Dupré's?'

After a quick look at Merten, Gastone nodded.

★ ★ ★ ★ ★

From time immemorial, the day of St. John the Baptist has been the event in the Fluentia calendar – being religious festival and Bacchanal at the same time. I may even have said this somewhere in my early Fluentia diary, but anyway: I did of course know it before Gastone reminded me of the day's imminence. The date is the 24th of June: when, according to legend, the Baptist first saw the light. Whatever woman yearned to be wedded: once a year, on the day of St. John the Baptist, her time had come, for the Baptist was believed to have the power of finding a husband for both widows and virgins. What I did not know is how people in the hills around Fluentia still revere the old customs.

As I am writing this down, I am indebted to Gastone for being much the wiser. He came to see me this morning. Today, needless to say, is the 23rd of June. In his own words, Gastone felt he owed me an explanation for the suggestion he made when we last met. He still hoped I would go up to the village underneath the monastery and join in the revelry, he said; 'but I want you to know, sir,' he added, 'what makes the locals tick.'

It is tonight, St. John's Eve, when the earth is supposed to open and yield both hidden treasures and waters which will grant their wish to those who hope for a long life. And it is tonight when people collect "the dew of St. John the Baptist": this dew will cure various evils, not least eye disease. It will also keep witches at bay. And as to witchcraft: if a mother, who believes her child to be – due to a spell – somehow abnormal, boils her offspring's clothes and keeps turning them over with forks, she will force the witch to come to her home and heal the child. It is actually St. John the Baptist who wills the witch to knock on the door of the house, three times and after the stroke of midnight. The operation, however, is not without danger; thus, the caring mother who initiates it risks excommunication!

This is what Gastone imparted upon me – and a few more pieces of intelligence which I thought about when later, down in Fluentia, I sat outside the café. Berenice came out and sat with me for a while. I mentioned my talk with the steward, and she immediately pointed in the direction of the temple of St. John the Baptist. Did I know that on this day – when Fluentia was still a republic – the entire square around the temple used to *be covered with painted cloths? If I walked around the square with an attentive eye, she told me, I would still detect traces of the fittings which held this artificial sky: iron fragments left in the facade of the cathedral and on many nearby houses. 'And of course tomorrow there will be far more people coming to the altar of St. John the Baptist with their offerings than on any other day of the year.' She shifted in her chair — the movement, which made me remember my very first chat with her at the till, was calculated to show off her long legs. 'What are you doing tonight, Leander?' I gave her a vague reply — but at the same time I told her about my imminent journey abroad, and that I had to prepare myself for it. 'Don't miss looking out for the bonfires from the windows of your villa,' she said. 'I hope I'll see more of you when you are back.' She got up and kissed me on my forehead — and then, circling the tables like a grand sailing ship, she disappeared through the entrance of the café. I had, by the way, briefly gone inside upon arriving; of course I had felt an urge to have a final look at the Samira fresco before setting out on my journey.*

I had known about the bonfires — and I looked out for the pyres when on my way back into the hills. Briefly, I thought of Brionnac, the place where my mother was born: how there, on the same day in June, the boy Leander Frédéric Merten used to marvel at the same kind of fire — lit on the plateau outside the church, from which, standing as I felt almost sky-high above the plain, I then believed I could see the whole world. It is remarkable how everywhere I have lived our ancestors credited the fire with even greater power than their prayers. If Gastone is right, the people in the villages are still convinced of its ability to heal — 'to combat,' in his own words, 'those evils which afflict humans, animals, even the fruit in our orchards. Evils spread by the demons of summer, creatures which ride through the air.' It is funny: when he talks about the weeping madonna, there is no doubt that he has no time for the whole thing. However, when it comes to pagan rituals — and beliefs associated with them — his own position is always less clear.

Anyway, small wonder the Eve of St. John the Baptist is still seen as a veritable nocturnal carnival. Back at Opaco and ascending the steps to the villa, I remembered how in heathen times humans used to be thrown into the bonfires by those who danced around them; later, animals were sacrificed — and only in a more civil age these victims were substituted by straw dolls. As I walked into the hall, my thoughts were interrupted by Amaranta. 'Would you mind very much, Leander, if I came in a little later tomorrow? I know you are leaving in the afternoon, but ...' — I told her that of course I did not mind. At the same time, a thought crossed my mind: I hoped she was not into this silly business of boiling her offspring's clothes during the night. I decided that, very soon, I had to talk to her about her son. She smiled, as if she had guessed what worried me. 'I only want to go to mass in the morning — as I usually do on the day of St. John the Baptist.' Shortly after, wishing me a good rest on the last night before my journey, she left.

Some four or five hours later, after I had eaten and packed my suitcase, I went up to the village. Intermittently, from all over the hills and out of the valley, the ringing of church bells reached my ears. Would the witches and demons take note? I looked up into the air. But then — just as I entered the village — I noticed the unmistakable smell of burning wood. It, and the noise the locals made, guided me in the direction of the bonfire. And what a merry crowd awaited me there! No doubt, the weeping madonna was, at least for a night, all but forgotten. It seemed that some people were dancing around the fire, but there were so many in front of me, just chatting and laughing, that apart from the occasional glimpse of bodies moving I could see nothing. Anyway, there were musicians playing. I wondered whether a straw doll had gone or would go up in the flames – and it occurred to me that whatever the villagers witnessed was probably derived from an ancient fertility rite. Like the ritual with the white dove which I had watched in Fluentia this was, for country folk, obviously the greater event even than the feast day it preceded. As I stood lost in thoughts, there was a stir in the crowd in front of me. Some people moved away from the bonfire, and I was able to claim a vantage point. There was indeed a group of men and women, hands linked, dancing around the fire. Amaranta was among them.

It was a frenzied dance, and eventually the dancers, one after the other, broke away to recover their breath. As some sat down and some chatted in little groups, I remembered what I had just read while, alone, having my dinner: that once upon a time, scenes from the Bible or mythological tales used to be performed in front of these bonfires. For instance the burning of Sodom and Gomorrah. I looked around to see where Amaranta was, but could not spot her. Maybe she was having a drink? But where? Just when I was about to move, the musicians started playing again. And there she was, in front of the fire. She started dancing all on her own. Again I looked around – surely, some man would join her. I remembered that another scene which, on the Eve of St. John the Baptist, used to be enacted in front of the bonfire was the story of Orpheus descending into the underworld to claim his beloved Eurydice. Amaranta was still dancing on her own. Yet everything behind and in front of her moved – the flames and her shadow, the latter at times almost reaching the spot where I stood. I stepped into the open space and walked up to her. The moment she recognized me, she stopped dead. I had never seen her so much at a loss. 'Dr. Merten' – she shook her head, correcting herself: 'Leander! What are you doing here?' I took her hand and said that I wanted to dance with her.

7

Of Paintings and Recipes

Merten first drove to the hamlet where his mother was buried. From there, as he stood in the churchyard, he looked up to Brionnac. Then he lowered his eyes and took count of the small number of crosses and slabs around him. He thought of how he had reacted when at Charlottenfels his mother first mentioned that this was to be her final resting place. In fact, he had never quite understood her choice while she was still alive. Her own country, yes. But why not in the very place where she grew up and had been happier than in all her married years? Why down here, a few miles only from Brionnac? He had no longer questioned her motives after that first talk, but one day he did take heart again. The tenderness in her voice had surprised him – and looking back, he knew she appreciated that he cared. 'I want to see Brionnac from where I am buried,' she had said – 'this is why.' His eyes travelled up all the way to the small town again – right up to where, on the plateau beyond the trees, the boy Leander Frédéric Merten used to survey what he then saw as the entire universe. Wonderful, he thought. And as he left the churchyard, he once more admired – as he often did since her death – his mother's wisdom.

Halfway up on the road to Brionnac, Merten passed a large but inconspicuous farmstead. And there, just beyond the buildings, was the upright stone. Again, he remembered his mother: how she had told her son of a wager between Christ and the devil. Whichever of the two, thus the latter had proposed as one day they met at Brionnac, managed to throw a piece of rock the farthest, would be the sole owner of all the land underneath the town. The devil won – but his stone, just as the castle that stood near it, had long vanished, whereas the piece of rock Christ had thrown was still rooted to the spot where it had touched the ground.

Merten knew that he owed his fertile imagination to the many stories his mother had told her child. His father, a difficult and taciturn man, was a realist. As the road entered the forest underneath Brionnac, he slowed down. He thought of the delicious wild mushrooms which used to grow here. Would he still be able to smell them? Just as he pulled down the window, he came to a small clearing on the left. The spot was bathed in sunlight, and Merten stopped abruptly. His memory peopled the clearing. On Sunday mornings, when they were at Brionnac, the family had always been complete; in fact it was his father – the recluse – who insisted that they all came down here. Because of the mushrooms. A man, a woman and a child, the latter proudly carrying a basket – but when he got out of his car, the sun had gone and with it the vision. The steep path which from here led up to the town was now overgrown. For a moment, Merten was tempted to undertake the rest of his journey on foot. Then, thinking of his suitcase, he went back to the car. He knew that, anyway, once he was up there, he would have to do the last bit on foot. Brionnac was a medieval town in which all traffic was banned. He thought that the term village would be more appropriate; in the last letter he had had from here, he was told that the population was now down to just a handful of people.

As the tourists still came, there still was an inn. Merten, who knew the place and the couple who ran it well, had booked a room there. He could not face sleeping in his mother's house, given that it had been uninhabited for so long; despite the good offices of the old woman who looked after it, he imagined everything to be covered with dust. Slowly, with his suitcase, he walked up the narrow, cobblestoned street underneath the ruined castle. Everything, the fortified gate and, beyond, the ancient market hall, looked as it always had. Inside the hall, Brionnac assizes had in the olden times occasionally been held. Merten, having arrived outside the inn, looked all round him. Another curiosity caught his eye. It had the appearance of a seat – and was called the stone of enfranchisement. Whoever, risking a prison sentence, was quick enough to perch himself on this stone, could according to an ancient law not be seized by the officers of the Lord of Brionnac.

After he had unpacked his suitcase, he went down to the restaurant and from there into the kitchen. It was an old ritual; when visiting Brionnac as an adolescent, he had always spent a lot of time talking to the innkeeper – who was also the chef – in the kitchen. The man's all-round knowledge was amazing. And Merten was not mistaken: his host even knew about the new picture at Chandio. In fact, there were a couple of new pictures – just as Merten had been told by Pepalmar. After all, the innkeeper said, Chandio had been one of the first châteaux on the Republic's list of private monuments; hence, after the state had acquired it, special efforts were made to restore everything to its former glory. Eventually, the state even bought some works of art that were thought to be complimentary to the collection of lovers, real and imaginary, of the nobleman who had once lived there. Merten wanted to ask more about the one picture because of which he had come, but there was a noise in the restaurant. He heard someone come into the kitchen and turned around.

'Leander!'

'Nona!'

When he embraced her, the old woman cried, and he too lost his composure for a moment. She had always looked after the house whilst his parents were at Charlottenfels. And although she was not much older than his mother – when they were both girls, they even sat in the same schoolroom for a couple of years – she had all his life been Nona to him.

In the early evening, he walked over to his mother's house. He was astonished at how neat the small garden looked. And the interior of the house as well – once inside, he was immediately under the spell of the place again. They had never known its exact age; but the lower part of the main building was at least five hundred years old. Merten went from room to room, past the walls. The various photographs showing his mother when young had always made him feel far more at home than, at Charlottenfels, the austerity of his father's tall, dark bookcases. Finally, he entered the room which, when he visited as an adolescent, had become his study. Nona had opened the shutters all over the house, and since the writing desk was right by the window, he eventually sat down. As the houses in this part of Brionnac stood close to each other, he only saw a part of the market hall from his chair. His eyes surveyed the few items on the desk. There were a couple of letters – he guessed he had, as he often did when leaving Brionnac, left them for another perusal on the occasion of his next visit. Official stuff, he thought, too much out of date now anyway. But then he noticed that the one on top was not opened. Nor was the one underneath – and the handwriting on this envelope, which had an unusual stamp, was familiar.

As he read the letter, the old woman, whom he had heard enter the house, came into the room.

'Why did you never send this to me, Nona?' He held up the envelope with the unusual stamp.

The old woman looked disconcerted – she told him she did not remember the letter; adding that maybe she had put it on the desk in anticipation of a visit of his and had then forgotten.

She hesitated. 'Why did you not come for so long, Leander?' she then asked softly.

'I know that I have been negligent,' he said. She looked sad, and he got up and gave her a tender hug.

When she left, he sat down again. When had he given his Brionnac address to the Fandango girl? The letter, written some five years previously, was by her. Merten thought he remembered that those few other letters she had sent him after her departure from Fluentia had either still reached him there or at Charlottenfels. But he was no longer sure and, anyway, this one was dated long after he had last read any message of hers. In it, she said that she had married the year of her return home – and also that soon after, she had become the mother of a little girl. Like herself, her daughter was called Silvana. She added this had been her husband's wish. The letter ended with the admission that she was not happy – and that she hoped he was. Would he please, she asked, write to her.

★ ★ ★ ★ ★

It was a cold morning when he left for Chandio – nothing suggested that it was already early summer. The open country struck him as more beautiful than ever; the road in front disappeared in what looked like a silver screen, above which he occasionally saw a roof or the wall of a building bathed in sunlight. There were only a very few villages in between Brionnac and his destination – nothing really to identify with, apart from a small, meandering river. This river had always fascinated Merten: how, whenever it seemed to touch the road, it instantly moved into the opposite direction again. Very playful, he thought. He could not even see the river clearly on this day. What he could see through the silver screen was sometimes a tree, sometimes a post, probably holding up a fence or something – shapes which more than once looked like people to him. He thought of how along this river one of the fiercest battles in human history had been fought. And how the abundant grass had been soaked in blood – how the invaders had set up traps, and how the thousands who came to the rescue of a besieged hilltop town were cut down ruthlessly. Healthy flesh, men as well as their horses, had been turned into pulp. It was said that sometimes, at dawn or dusk, the victims' ghosts could be seen, rising from the river banks. Eventually, with the sun becoming stronger, the veil evaporated. And as he drove on, his eye kept following the course of the river. His conclusion was the same as many times before: he had never beheld a more peaceful sight.

When he took the secondary road to Chandio, he looked out for the monument to the local chieftain which he knew was visible in the distance to his left – allegedly the man, a hero who, to save his people, had given himself up to the invaders, was strangled after seven years of captivity. As the road required his full attention, he failed to spot the monument on high. And the closer he got to Chandio, the more he thought of a different kind of hero. The count whose creation the château – more precisely: its interior decoration – was, had been not only one of the most gallant men, but probably the greatest shot of his age. A first-rate soldier, anyway. How could such a man content himself with looking at his lovers' pictures only? Not all the ladies of the court had given the count their likeness, but when Merten had last visited the château, twenty-seven portraits hung on the notorious man's bedroom walls. Nine of these ladies were immortalized in the scandalous publication which caused its author's banishment to here. To the provinces. When he was a child, Merten had always been hit by the isolation of Chandio – now, as he pulled up outside, the place struck him as the embodiment of a present day Arcadia. So what was different in his childhood – or indeed in the count's days? In the latter's case, it was a question of honour and reputation. How much did such principles matter today? The tragedy of no longer being a courtier: that was what made the count seek refuge in a bedroom with, on its walls, the great ladies of his age.

Merten had spoken to the administrator's secretary on the telephone. He had told her that he was in the process of writing a book on a group of frescoes – and that he had heard that a fresco which was essential to the research he was still engaged in was now at Chandio. The lady had been most obliging. When she mentioned the administrator's name, he realized that a new man was in charge; hence, to make it easier for them, he emphasized that he was not a first time visitor.

Both secretary and administrator waited for him in the latter's office.

'I hear you already know the château,' the administrator, who had probably graduated only a few years ago, said.

Merten answered in the affirmative. He admitted to his Brionnac connection – strangely his mother's name, a country girl's really, had always carried far more weight than his well-connected father's.

The administrator's eyes lit up. 'My father still talks about your mother and I saw her a couple of times when I was a child. My father,' he added, 'was the notary at neighbouring Rabussin.'

Merten remembered the man – at one time a great support to his mother in some legal business – and said so. The administrator seemed pleased. Then he made an inviting gesture: should they go and see the fresco straight away?

Everything in the count's private apartment was as Merten remembered. Antechamber, chamber – and from there, through the windows, the view onto the wing with gallery and chapel. But it was the salon he was interested in – which, given the central piece of furniture in it, had in his memory always been the bedroom. As they were about to enter, he told the administrator of his many visits as a youth. Again he realized how indebted he was to his mother – it was she who, when he was a small and impressionable boy, started taking him here.

The administrator seemed to have guessed his thought. 'May I say,' he remarked as they walked into the salon, 'how much I admired your mother. What an elegant lady!'

Merten smiled. What mattered most was personality; not, he thought of his father, connections. Nor titles – such as his own, however hard he had worked for it.

When he looked up to the ceiling, his reflective mood changed instantly. There, his expensively trained eye told him, was the real thing. The shape was oval – and the portrait of a woman surrounded by putti flying through the air and tumbling on the floor was indeed by a gifted artist. 'Samira, mistress of the second Grand Duke of Fluentia,' he said to himself.

'I beg your pardon?' The administrator looked nonplussed.

Merten smiled. 'I am just completing the information given in your commendable visitors' guide.' He once more looked at the small booklet in his hands. 'She had indeed once been a courtesan, your Fluentia beauty,' he then added. 'It just happens that I have done a lot of research on this particular fresco – or rather on one that bears a strong resemblance to it and is still in Fluentia.'

He looked up to the ceiling again. Samira's hair – as on the cover of the book which had first provided him with her identity – was reddish. He studied the picture for a while;

then he looked straight at the administrator. 'I suppose you – I mean the state – acquired this portrait from a private collector?' he ventured.

The administrator said he thought so; but he was not absolutely sure, as he had not yet been in his post at the time. 'My father, in his professional capacity, was marginally involved. I am sure he knows some more details. He still lives at Rabussin – and if I tell him who you are, he would be ever so pleased to see you.'

They decided to call the old notary and went back to the administrator's office. Soon after, Merten was on his way to Rabussin.

'Leander!' The old man held out both his hands. 'Do you mind if I still call you Leander?'

'Of course not. On the contrary!' Merten was moved; again, his warm reception was due to the strength of memory.

They sat down, and once more Merten was surprised at how much his father was a nonentity when the older people remembered his family's stays at Brionnac. He felt bad to have to remind his host after a while why he had come.

The notary nodded. 'I can't tell you much, Leander – I did not negotiate any of these acquisitions, I only gave my son's predecessor, who was a friend, the occasional piece of advice.' He went quiet, obviously thinking very hard. 'The vendor of the Fluentia beauty? I do remember the people who delivered the picture, but I guess that's not enough. One was a curator or something – perhaps the custodian of a church. He was quite elderly. And the other one just seemed this man's porter: a stocky fellow – with a rather well-proportioned head, though.'

Merten had heard enough. That Cesini had made it to Chandio did not surprise him. What surprised him was the absence of Dupré. And that instead of this puppet-master, the largely invisible sacristan had turned up. But then the latter seemed to travel as much as Dupré – at least this was what, at Opaco, Gastone's comment had implied.

Before he left, the notary told him that the former administrator of the château was dead. And also that the records of acquisitions by the state were all kept in some central archive where, it was said, no one ever found anything.

On his way back to Brionnac, Merten put what he suspected and what he now knew to be fact into chronological order. Cesini had probably, maybe on the orders of Dupré, substituted the original Samira portrait with a copy of his own when as a young man he first restored the frescoes in the Fluentia café. Either the restorer, or Dupré, had sat on the stolen original for years, because, as it was associated with the history of Fluentia in that city's heyday, it would not be easy to sell. Around the time when he became a regular guest in the café – courtesy of Strange Fruit, Merten thought with amusement – they were probably negotiating with the château at Chandio. They would by then have concluded that to sell the picture to a provincial collection in another country, rather than to a famous museum, was the smallest risk – even if they had to accept less money for it. He remembered the telephone conversation which Amaranta had overheard: how Cesini told Dupré he was afraid that he, Merten, would 'find out.' So that was why Cesini, who had originally produced a very good likeness of the Samira fresco, gradually added touches that made the portrayed lady look different. But why did he make her resemble Amaranta, his then ex-wife? Merten knew that Amaranta knew, as she had said she could not possibly tell him. He would have to ask her again as soon as he was back in Fluentia. But whatever her answer and, more importantly, even if his hypothesis was entirely correct:

how could he ever produce all the evidence needed to have Dupré and Cesini locked up? He had just joined the main road to Brionnac again; and as usual along this road, the at one time blood-soaked fields and the peacefully meandering river claimed his attention.

★ ★ ★ ★ ★

Back at Brionnac, he lay awake most of the night. He could not banish the Samira portrait from his mind. Nor, as hard as he tried, the thought of another woman. When coming up through the fortified gate and walking into the square with the market hall, he had bumped straight into Nona. 'Somebody has telephoned and wanted to talk to you,' she had said unceremoniously.

'Who?' he enquired.

'A lady. But I did not understand her well. She spoke with a foreign accent – she had a striking, rather deep voice.'

Merten identified the caller immediately; and, as he lay awake, he realized for the first time since his Strange Fruit days how badly he wanted her body to be near to his. Despite their dancing on the eve of St. John the Baptist, they had both been reserved for the rest of that evening. And Amaranta was equally restrained when, after mass, she had come back to the villa on the morning of his departure.

He had finally fallen asleep and was late for breakfast. As there were no other guests, he walked straight into the kitchen, where his host was busy preparing the lunchtime menu of the day. Merten asked whether he could help himself to some bread and cheese.

'Of course. And try this – I have just made it.' The innkeeper pushed a jug towards him. 'It's a fruit juice mix. Everything in it comes from the trees in our own orchard and from the forest of Brionnac.'

Merten had always loved to sample the man's latest recipes.

'Have you already seen our church?' the innkeeper asked as he sipped his drink. It had been Merten's intention to go there after breakfast, and he said so. 'You will like the wall paintings, Leander. They were restored three years ago.'

'Really? It was about time. You know that I had always maintained those colours should not have been left in their poor, faded condition.' When still an adolescent, Merten had once campaigned for a full-scale restoration of the paintings, but with no success.

'It was not their condition which prompted the state to intervene,' his host remarked. 'Five years ago, we had an unusually hot summer – and suddenly, the red paint on two of the frescoes started to liquefy. It looked eerie, like blood trickling down the walls.'

'Are you joking?' Merten felt a strange thrill.

The innkeeper laughed. 'Well, both the locals and some of the more perceptive visitors to Brionnac were a bit puzzled initially. But when the inspector of national monuments came for the first time, he brought with him the country's most acclaimed restorer. And it was this chap who explained that to achieve a certain effect, some painters in the past had concocted gels by availing themselves of naturally occurring reddish chemicals such as iron chloride, or had used fats and waxes which they would colour with a dash of devil's blood, a fat-soluble red vegetable resin. The only trouble with such concoctions was that if shaken or reaching high temperatures, they were likely to liquefy.'

'Great!' Merten, although stunned, spontaneously felt that what he had just been told merited applause.

His host was amused. 'Don't tell me this is all news to you, the art historian?'

'It is. They may award doctorates, but they don't teach you such things at the arts faculty.' He told the innkeeper about the weeping madonna in the village above Opaco. 'Do you think somebody could have improved on the formula used at Brionnac – I mean: to produce fake blood?'

The innkeeper laughed. 'It is the easiest thing in the world to make fake blood – don't forget,' he added, 'that I am a cook.' Merten said that he would be most happy to be introduced to yet another of his host's recipes. 'Just grind some digestive biscuits and add cranberry juice. Your blood may be a bit congealed, though. If you want it runny, you can use washing-up liquid as a base, or golden syrup. Even a dash of coffee works well.' His host looked at him. 'Let's just do it, shall we?'

The experiment was a brief, but fascinating lesson. Afterwards, his visit to the church – where the restored wall paintings looked indeed spectacular – and a subsequent walk helped Merten clear his head. He stopped outside his mother's house and spent most of the remaining day there, going from room to room. Lingering here and there, he realized that he would have to come back soon and go through everything that was left in the cupboards, chests and up in the attics. Finally, he telephoned Amaranta.

'I didn't know you spoke foreign languages – you were the caller, weren't you?' he said without announcing himself.

She sounded surprised and pleased to hear him. Yes, she said – 'Professor Pepalmar rang, saying he has arranged a day for a meeting between the two of you and a friend he had spoken to you about. It's next week.' She paused. 'Oh, the language! Well, my grandfather – after whom Davide is named – was a native of your mother's country. He paid for me to have private lessons.' Merten complimented her on her talents, and she laughed. 'Thank you. I wish I had stood up to both my grandfather's and my father's expectations.' There was another pause. 'When are you coming back, Leander?'

'Tomorrow,' he said, 'with the morning flight.'

She was chattier than usual, telling him all sorts of things – about the villa, about what her son had done in the garden, and about her own home. He said he was looking forward to seeing her the day after, and, instead of going quiet as he expected, she reacted with obvious pleasure.

'By the way: has the madonna wept blood again?'

Amaranta said she had; and that Cesini was doing better business than ever, selling his replicas. 'How come you bought one?' she wanted to know – 'I only saw it yesterday, when telephoning Brionnac from the desk in your study, where you had left your number.' He gave her the same evasive reply he had given Gastone. But then he admitted he had had an ulterior motive. He said he would tell her more when he was back at Opaco. She asked whether he had made arrangements for transport from the airport. He said no, but that he intended to take a train to Fluentia and from there a taxi to Opaco.

When a little later Merten locked the house and went back to the inn, there was about an hour left before dinner time. He decided to pack his suitcase straight away. It was a quick job – and just before he finished, he reached for his jacket and pulled out the letter by the Fandango girl, which he had pocketed before leaving his mother's house. He put it on top of everything and closed the case. When he went down to the restaurant, the Samira portrait was on his mind again. He knew that, given the time which had passed since the removal of the original fresco from the ceiling of the Fluentia café, he had little chance of nailing Dupré and Cesini. And that crook of a sacristan! Unless … unless he could prove that they were also the masterminds behind the weeping madonna business and, to begin with, that the whole thing was a hoax.

8

The Temperature Rises

As he was sitting on the aeroplane, he thought of his diary. He felt it was about time to take up his pen and start a new page – but there was no inner voice telling him what to put onto paper. He tried to remember his entries so far; and as his memory had always been exceptional, he managed without much effort. And while mentally rehearsing, he realized why he had dried up. Although intended to contrast with the flowery attempt of his early Fluentia days, his Opaco diary was really just an extension of those first outpourings. It was again the fantastic, the things that seemed beyond belief, which had inspired his forays into first person narrative. As that grand old man of letters visiting his parents at Charlottenfels had once said: writing was a way of coming to grips with experiences which were unusual. But now, after Chandio and Rabussin and – at Brionnac – his initiation into the art of a professional cook, everything seemed clear as daylight.

It also occurred to him now that, after one or two tentative appearances, Amaranta had suddenly moved centre stage in the diary. What on earth had prompted him to bring her in? With her, it dawned upon him, reality had asserted itself; a reality he would have to face before dealing with all the other – now threateningly realistic – issues. Hence: farewell to the diary – farewell to all that had seemed fantastic. He looked out of the window for a while and noticed how the hills he saw far below were beginning to look familiar. As the plane started its descent, Merten knew that for a number of people, himself included, life would soon be different. Yet, he also knew that he would soon feel an urge to re-read his Opaco notes. Not as an exercise in escapism; but rather – again he remembered his Charlottenfels lesson – as an ultimate, although indirect attempt to get a grip on what was clearly not the work of Satanists but of a gang of moneymaking frauds.

★ ★ ★ ★ ★

When he walked into the arrivals hall, he was surprised to see Gastone.

'What a welcome,' he said; 'how come you knew my flight details – not to speak of having the time to pick me up?'

The steward gave him a broad smile. 'Well, sir, Amaranta informed and urged me – she says you don't seem to realize that you are still supposed to take things easy. Anyway, who could resist such a woman's appeal?' Merten was both touched and in agreement. Gastone took his suitcase. 'You know she has just passed her driving test – she actually wanted to take your car and come down here herself, but I thought that was a bit wild. She is, with respect, a wild child of nature – at the steering wheel just as in all other things.' Merten had to laugh aloud. Not only his affection for Amaranta, but also his sympathy for the steward was stirred. 'Don't get me wrong, sir: I hold the lady in question in high esteem.' Merten assured Gastone he had no doubt. At the same time, it struck him how little he still knew of Amaranta – no matter how frank she was whenever he asked her a question. Although he had never seen her with a car, he was amazed to learn that she did not even drive until recently.

On the road to Opaco, after some general talk, it was Gastone who broached the subject which was foremost in Merten's mind. 'Mr. Dupré must have been astonished when he found out whom you had employed as your housekeeper, sir – given the landlord's close and somewhat enigmatic associations with Amaranta's former husband.'

Merten shrugged his shoulders and explained that of course he had no clue of who was who, who knew whom and in what way. 'How long have you known Mr. Dupré?' he then asked.

'Oh, for ages,' Gastone replied. 'Before me, my father had been the steward of the winemaking co-operative; and he had also looked after the villa, which was then under different ownership. But Dupré already owned the house behind the church and was therefore a neighbour. Mind you, we didn't see much of him. Anyway, Dupré bought the villa a few years after I had taken over as steward, and I guess he just saw it as the most convenient thing that I should continue to look after the big house.

'I am glad you do,' Merten said.

'And I, whatever Mr. Dupré's opinion may be, am pleased with whom you have chosen as the lady of your castle,' the steward replied. What an extraordinary figure of speech, Merten thought – and he said so. 'Well, sir, Amaranta is greatly appreciated by the locals in the surrounding villages, and you do need this kind of person to run your house – especially when you are absent. Besides, she is known as a great cook, which I think is the best guarantee for someone convalescent.'

Merten said he was quite aware of her qualities – 'but if Amaranta has, as you say, a reputation for her cooking, I do wonder why she didn't make this her profession.'

'Maybe I shouldn't say this, sir, but she did after a glorious start have quite a messy – perhaps the kinder word is unorthodox – spell in her life.'

Merten indicated that he knew something. 'Do tell me about the glorious start, though!'

'As a little girl,' the steward said, 'Amaranta showed a strong interest in dancing. Her father was very musically orientated and arranged for her to have tuition. Eventually, she was foretold a future as a great ballerina. Her father, who at the time owned the bar in the village underneath the monastery, was delirious – he hired a famous *maître de ballet*. But then, after a few acclaimed appearances on stage when still less than sixteen, she met Cesini and started hanging about with him. Her father continued to pay the *maître de ballet* – but as this had always been beyond his means, he finally went bankrupt and had to start working as a waiter down in Fluentia.'

Merten had become thoughtful. Why had he never even guessed? The way she moved! He also remembered St. John's Eve: how, almost frantically, she had danced on her own – and how the flames behind her had highlighted the spectacle. As he had been quiet, the steward looked at him questioningly – and he responded with an encouraging nod.

'You seem constantly on her mind, sir. Whenever I met her, since you left, she only talked about you. I mean: about your requirements and what she thinks is good for you – perhaps that's why I called her the lady of your castle.'

'What is all this talk about Alpiniano's Court?' Merten asked. 'I mean: how come that this is the name you use when referring to Mr. Dupré's house?'

High above them, the villa had come in sight and Gastone, who not only drove fast but negotiated the bends with obvious relish, kept his eyes steadily on the road. 'Maybe it is just a whim of mine, sir,' he finally said – 'but I know Mr. Dupré is greatly taken with the idea of a mystery surrounding his place. Or even his person. But I cannot say more, because I have little to do with him. I may add that I deeply dislike his entourage. I mean Cesini and the sacristan – and that obnoxious marshal, by the way, is a buddy of theirs. No doubt Mr. Dupré is aware of my feelings.' For a moment, Gastone took his eyes off the road and looked at Merten.

'Just in case,' Merten said, 'you are still in doubt: I share your feelings.' The steward's grin – his eyes were back on the road – indicated that he had expected the reply. 'We must keep exchanging notes,' Merten added; 'I too am taken with the mystery of Alpiniano's Court.'

There was a long silence between them. As Gastone turned off the main road and drove up towards the winemaking co-operative, he told Merten that it was said that Dupré occasionally organised medieval banquets at his place – 'but I have no idea as to who the guests are, or even what the scenario is.'

As they got out of the car, Gastone offered to carry the suitcase over to the villa, but Merten declined. The steward looked at him, pointing at the same time to the buildings next to them. 'You are a regular customer of ours, sir – but what your excellent housekeeper does not know is that we also make a very special wine. Only a few hundred bottles a year. Would you allow me to welcome you back with one of these special bottles?' Without waiting for an answer, he gave orders to one of the workers who, as always, were busy in the forecourt of the co-operative.

After he had been given his welcome gift, Merten walked slowly over to the villa. As usual, the entrance being at the back, he had to cross part of the garden and therefore had occasion to notice the work Amaranta's son had done. He was wondering whether she had seen him approach. And when he came round the corner, there she was: at the top of the steps, looking spectacular. Black trousers, a broad belt and a black top – and over the top a short, dark-red jacket. Her hair was shorter again, but he liked it that way. Quite an amazon, he thought. When he put his foot on the first step, he remembered the emperor who went to Canossa – he felt he was in a similarly reflective mood. She started coming down, but he was already halfway up. When he reached the step underneath her, he let go of his suitcase.

Going down on one knee, he held out Gastone's rare bottle with both hands. 'Sir Leander greets the Lady of the Castle,' he said; 'and he begs her to celebrate his return with him.'

She laughed more merrily than ever since he had known her. 'Leander, what has got into you!'

He put down the bottle and stood up. 'You,' he said; 'a long time ago.' She had taken his hands, but seemed to freeze slightly when she realized that he was serious. He took her in his arms and kissed her. 'Isn't this a great setting, my lady,' he said with a sweeping gesture. And when he kissed her again, she yielded.

★ ★ ★ ★ ★

The morning after, he exercised himself on his bicycle again. Amaranta had been right: this was not quite his style. He would have preferred to go running in the woods – but when after his arrival at Opaco before Easter he had taken a long walk, he had come face to face with some ferocious dogs. Eventually, their owner had materialised; but he knew – as usual, Gastone was his source – that his had not been a chance encounter. The few wealthy people in the hills who needed such beasts to protect their estates would, when walking them, let them off the leash as soon as they felt they were out of sight. No, he once more said to himself, he did not want to risk another such adventure. And to judge from how Davide eyed it, his bicycle was a fine machine. He had decided even before his journey to Brionnac that on the day he left for good Amaranta's son would get the bike.

Whenever that would be. Although, when he went for a ride, he had intended to focus on his meeting with the district attorney – he had telephoned the man straight after breakfast – he could not keep Amaranta out of his thoughts. The celebration between Sir Leander and the Lady of the Castle had ended most passionately. As Gastone had said: she was a wild child of nature. And very much so in the bedroom. Now, his at one time obsession with her physical attributes struck Merten as sadly one-dimensional – the body and the personality, or rather the personality and the body: this was what accounted, indeed was the formula, for her enormous appeal. At some stage, she had gone quiet, and he thought she had fallen asleep. But her eyes were wide open. 'Berenice Miolane rang while you were away,' she said. He waited for what was to come. 'She sounded very possessive.' He nodded slowly – 'I know. It's her biggest drawback.' She looked at him intently. 'Do I have to share you with her, Leander? She is, by the way, quite exceptional.' He laughed. 'Yes, I suppose she is. But the answer you want is no – I am not in the habit of being shared.' She still looked at him searchingly. 'You once,' he said, 'told me that when after your father's death you moved in with Cesini again, you just needed a man in the house.' She nodded. 'Well, I guess that after months of feeling like a vegetable I needed company and warmth when this spring I arrived back in Fluentia.' Her eyes had become very big, but he could read agreement in them. 'Besides, you – and let me tell you that at times I could hardly keep my hands off you – were always so reserved. Why, Amaranta?' His confession produced an obvious thrill, but her reply was very measured. 'I just needed this job, Leander. Very badly.' For a little while, he caressed her gently. She took his hand and pressed her warm body against his. And then she had fallen asleep.

The fresh air had been good for him – in an hour or so it would be hot. Back at the villa, he put his bicycle into the storeroom underneath the steps. He needed to change for his meeting with the district attorney down in Fluentia. When he walked through the entrance and into the hall, Amaranta came down the stairs from the upper floor. She looked radiant and this time he waited for her to say something.

'Are you off to see the attorney?' she asked. He had telephoned from the hall after breakfast, which was why she knew. He answered in the affirmative, and her expression instantly became serious. She put her arms around his neck – 'Why do you want to talk to him, Leander?'

'I shall tell you later today. Provided you are still here when I come back.'

She said that if he was late, she would, like on some previous occasions, leave a light meal on the table for him. 'But I want to see you,' she added; 'hence, I shall come back after I have cooked for Davide.'

'Have you got transport?' he asked.

'Yes,' she said proudly. 'Didn't you see that wonderful little Fiat outside the co-operative? It's mine! Honestly: the model is ancient. But a neighbour gave it to me for nothing – and this morning the mechanic I paid to give it an overhaul brought it here.'

Merten had seen the Fiat and said that with her inside it was no doubt the most desirable car north of Fluentia. Shortly after, having changed, he left for his meeting.

The district attorney's name was Talon. On the telephone Merten, identifying himself as an art historian recently arrived at Opaco, had only mentioned that he would like to pass on some information possibly in connection with the weeping madonna. And on the road to Fluentia, he decided it was pointless, at this stage, to say much about the fresco in the café and his visit to Chandio. To begin with, he had no photographs to prove the twofold transformation the lady presently portrayed on the ceiling of the café had undergone. Furthermore, he had no documents attesting the sale through Cesini and the sacristan of the portrait that was now at Chandio – and he also had no proof of this portrait having originally been in the Fluentia café, when Cesini first started restoring the frescoes there. The old notary at Rabussin would most likely recognize both Cesini and the sacristan. But this had to wait. For the moment he would, as he had already concluded on his last night at Brionnac, have to focus on the question marks over the weeping madonna.

'It is most kind of you to come and see me, Dr. Merten!'

The district attorney was younger than he had guessed – probably about his own age, Merten thought. After they had sat down, the attorney wanted to know what had brought him to Opaco. The man, Merten soon decided, was both a good listener and highly intelligent – one of those rare persons who know what someone is going to say the moment he or she has uttered a few words. Hence, having divulged some autobiographical details, he came straight to the point. He told Talon what he knew about red paint liquefying, and also about producing fake blood. The district attorney was mesmerised.

'May I know,' Merten asked, 'whether you think that when you had the statue examined at Fluentia University the scientists there did a thorough job?'

'Absolutely,' Talon replied; 'I was present myself.'

'Was this immediately after one of the weeping episodes?'

Talon smiled approvingly. 'No,' he said, 'a couple of days later. Are you suggesting, Dr. Merten, that somebody could in the meantime have exchanged the statue for a replica – or have applied some real blood to its cheeks before it was taken down to Fluentia? Or both?'

This time it was Merten's turn to indicate approval. 'Exactly!' He hesitated. 'I suppose you know that up at Opaco there is a man selling replicas of the madonna to tourists?'

'Sure.' The attorney waited.

'Well, I may as well tell you that there are two or three individuals up there whom I have reason to suspect of forgery – in fact even of selling stolen artworks abroad. But I am still short of some of the circumstantial evidence.' He was tempted to say more – but instead, he rose.

Again, Talon understood instinctively. He too got up. 'Well, Dr. Merten, all I can say is that I have great confidence in your professional views. I do hope to see you again before long.'

Merten said the feeling was mutual. The district attorney interested him – like in the case of Pepalmar, he felt that there was an affinity between him and the man.

An hour later, he sat outside the café. Berenice had joined him at his table. She said she wanted him to tell her about his trip – about this château he had briefly mentioned. She admitted she had telephoned his villa; but his housekeeper, she added, seemed to know very little.

'She only mentioned a place called Brionnac.'

He was about to say that he had not discussed his trip with anyone when he felt that somebody had walked up to them from behind. He turned round and beheld the owner of his villa.

Dupré smiled. 'How is your health, Dr. Merten?' Still smiling, he addressed Berenice: 'Can't you stop him from travelling when he is supposed to recuperate?'

'How come you know?' Merten asked before Berenice could say anything.

'I too met somebody at the airport yesterday – and the moment I spotted Gastone you walked into the arrivals hall.'

Merten assured Dupré that his health was fine; adding that he would probably before long undertake another journey.

'His health is so good,' Berenice quipped, 'that he doesn't have time for me – he prefers visiting places nobody has heard of. Have you,' she asked Dupré, 'ever been to Brionnac?'

'She thinks she is being funny,' Merten said.

'Or,' Berenice cut in again, 'to some château in the Brionnac area?'

It was obvious that Dupré did not consider the questions as funny. In spite of the heat, the man looked frozen. But the smile did return, and Dupré even put a fatherly hand on Merten's shoulder. 'I have to take leave,' he said – 'no doubt our adorable friend Berenice has a right to claim your undivided attention.'

'Are you staying with me tonight?' she asked as soon as Dupré had gone.

'No,' he said – adding, after a pause, that he would continue to be a guest in the café, but not in her private apartment.

He had not misjudged her: her pride got the better of her, and rather than throw a tantrum she leaned back elegantly and, putting her hand under her chin, waited for him to say more. He only mentioned that he had suddenly become involved with someone whom, ironically, he had known for a very long time. 'Still seeing you would mean being unfair to two unusual ladies.'

She laughed. 'Thanks for the compliment, Leander. I always knew you were dangerous. You don't compromise – for you, things are either black or white.' Her assessment was a direct hit. He was going to say something to the effect, but she silenced him by briefly putting her hand on his. 'By the way,' she said, 'I was very surprised when I realized who your housekeeper is.'

This time it was his turn to laugh. 'So was I – I had not recognized her when she came for the job interview.'

Berenice gave him a questioning look, but he did not want to enlarge. 'Amaranta is an exceptional lady,' she finally said.

He smiled. 'Incidentally,' he remarked, 'she says the same about you.'

Soon after, he was back at Opaco. As it was early evening, he knew that Amaranta had left – and when he heard the telephone ring, he ran up the steps to unlock the front door and answer it.

'Where the hell have you been?' The caller was Pepalmar. 'And who the hell is the woman in your house? Her voice is enticing, I must say – do, please, introduce me to her!'

Merten was greatly amused. So Pepalmar still did not know who his housekeeper was. 'She may be too old for you, my dear Professor,' he ventured – 'she looks more than twenty to me.'

As his friend was easily flattered and also had a good sense of humour, the words did the trick and provoked the usual musical, good-natured laugh. 'But tell me, Leander,' the professor then said: 'why is it me supplying you with women and not the other way round?'

For a moment, Merten thought the lady in the fresco at Chandio was meant. However, Pepalmar became specific – he said that his contact at Fluentia University, the lady who had spotted Merten on Easter Saturday, was free the day after. 'And as I am having a few people around, I asked her to join us. Are you available, by any chance?' Merten said he was.

Having accepted Pepalmar's invitation, he went into the dining room. His light meal was on the table, with a note from Amaranta. He checked his watch. She would be back in an hour. Remembering that he had still not unpacked his suitcase, he decided to go upstairs at once. Stowing away his things did not take him long. It amazed him, though, that he had completely forgotten about the letter with the unusual stamp. But did he really want to reply? The writer had been unhappy when, years ago, she penned her message – but perhaps she was happy now? Anyway, the letter had slumbered amidst things past at Brionnac. Merten concluded that this was what destiny had wanted. Having put the letter in a drawer which contained things dealt with, he went downstairs again. He was still sitting at the dining table when he heard a car drive into the forecourt of the winemaking co-operative. A few moments later, the door opened and Amaranta burst into the room.

'I have just made this for Davide – and I thought you would like it as well.' She put a piece of cake in front of him.

He was moved and drew her to him. Although it was obvious that she wanted to be caressed, she soon freed herself and sat down.

'Tell me why you bought one of Cesini's statues. And why you went to see the district attorney.' She shifted in her seat and took both his hands. 'You were going to tell me, Leander, weren't you? And why did you go to Brionnac?'

He looked at her. 'It is a long story, but I shall try to make it short. It all has to do with what I questioned you about before: the fresco in the café.' Merten told her what he had not told the district attorney. In the end he added what he knew about faking blood, and also about red paint liquefying. 'I do think that Dupré and Cesini are, so to speak, on rather intimate terms with the weeping madonna.'

Leaning back in their chairs, they had both moved slightly apart. But she laughed when he made his last comment.

'These two have been on intimate terms with better works of art – as indeed you have just implied. What you don't know, Leander, is why I finally kicked Cesini out. I know he deserved the boot long before, but anyway: he was investigated after a flower painting he had restored was declared by an expert to be a cocktail of flowers from a variety of works by different artists. The investigators could prove very little and certainly had no case against him. I, however, had overheard fragments of telephone conversations between Cesini and Dupré, which made it easy for me to put two and two together. And this is why I decided that I no longer wanted to have anything to do with a man who, although perhaps only a minor crook himself, was the associate of some big time crooks.'

Their evening ended in the bedroom. When, after a while, the wild child of nature and former ballet dancer said that she would have to go home, he shook his head.

'Not yet,' he said. 'So far tonight, you have asked all the questions – but I have a question too.' She turned onto her stomach and looked at him intently. 'Do you remember when we talked about how the fresco in the café suddenly resembled you? I asked you then what explanation Cesini had to offer.' He tried to imitate her voice. '*I can't possibly tell you, Dr. Merten – Leander*' ... this is what you said. You also said that Cesini had declared he hoped to have played a trick on me. But why did he not just change the portrait – why did he make the courtesan resemble you?

This time, she was amused rather than embarrassed. Yet, she did not answer immediately. And when she did – she was still lying on her stomach – she turned her head to look at her own body. 'Well, *Dr. Merten*, don't forget that I had told you Cesini had at the time become quite crazy about me again. And he said he thought, having watched you in the café, that you were obsessed with that – again she looked over her shoulder – with that big bottom of mine. At the time, I thought it was just one of Cesini's weird ideas – I didn't really consider the fresco issue, Leander.'

He put his hand on the formidable shape in question and told her that Cesini was a wonderfully perceptive man. 'Obsessed is too mild a term – and, by the way, I still am.'

She laughed and said she was happy that her body gave him pleasure.

It was very late when he heard her little Fiat leave the forecourt of the winemaking co-operative.

★ ★ ★ ★ ★

The day after, he was slightly late for Pepalmar's lunchtime do. When he walked into the house, he was surprised at the number of people in the two front rooms. He introduced himself to some of them, but the noise made conversation difficult and he started looking out for the host. As he turned round, he saw a youngish, very elegant woman on a chair near the door he had just walked through. He went over and greeted her as well.

'Merten,' he said; 'Leander Merten.'

She looked at him for a moment and then, with a hardly perceptible smile, held out her hand. 'I am Sylvie,' she said.

She had beautiful eyes, he thought – the sort of eyes he could get lost in. After a few courtesies, he excused himself; he said he was still looking for their host. But at this instant, Pepalmar walked up to them.

'I am glad you two have found each other,' the professor said, and the two men embraced.

Merten said he was glad too – 'but do tell me: where is that friend of yours I am supposed to meet? The one who recognized me on Easter Saturday.'

Pepalmar looked nonplussed. 'Have you gone crazy? It's her!' The professor pointed to the lady in the chair.

Was he, Merten asked himself, perhaps missing something?

'I am sorry, Sylvie' he said to the woman: it seems we have met before.'

Her smile had become more than just perceptible. 'Indeed,' she said – and, after a pause: 'it also seems that you have become rather formal, Leander.'

'The man is impossible!,' Pepalmar shouted; 'you know, he excels at recognizing pictures – but when it comes to people, he is obviously hopeless.'

'Just formal,' she said; 'it's that Charlottenfels place which has done it to him: going back to where he grew up.' She was laughing now. 'Would you believe how he introduced himself to me? Merten, he said; Leander Merten.' She turned round and looked straight at Merten. 'Maybe I should do likewise?'

These eyes, he thought again: almond-shaped – with now a slightly roguish expression in them. In a split second, he knew what was coming. He felt the floor go under his feet.

'Fandango,' she said; 'Silvana Fandango.'

Hours later, when he was on the road to Opaco again, he could not remember any of the other guests at Pepalmar's. Meeting La Fandango unexpectedly, after all these years, had been too much. And there had been too many exchanges and explanations between them – there was, not least, her letter he had found at Brionnac not more than a week ago. Although her hair had changed from auburn to a Titian red, she was amazed that he had not recognized her; but she believed him when he said that if it had not been for the noise made by the other guests, her voice would instantly have put him on the right track. She had asked him about his health – she had heard from Pepalmar about his operation. He had asked her how she was: whether she was happier now. Yes, she said; she had left her husband, which was why she was back in

Fluentia. She hesitated. Her health, she added slowly, was another matter. It struck him then that she had not for a moment risen from her chair. She had had a second child, she said – a boy. Already before his birth, she had found walking increasingly difficult, and she had felt increasing abdominal pain. This did not resolve itself after delivery. She was told it was all due to a hormone produced during pregnancy, which led to a softening of the ligaments of the pelvis. It did not happen very often – but it had conditioned her to spending half of the day in a wheelchair. She said that a few hours of teaching and taking visiting foreign academics around Fluentia University was just about the maximum she could do, standing on her legs. 'But tell me about you, Leander,' she had wanted to know; 'our host has told me that you are not married – but are you with someone who cares?' He heard himself say that he was. 'It's a rather new relationship,' he then added – 'although with somebody I first met shortly after you had left. Pepalmar doesn't know about it. The lady is my housekeeper at Opaco. She is quite wonderful in how she looks after me – and she is in your league of great-looking women.' Silvana said she was happy for him. And he, on the road to Opaco, was happy he had finally mentioned Amaranta to someone who mattered. He realized it sort of legitimised the woman he was no longer just obsessed, but probably also in love with. It was even later than the night before, when, in his villa, he heard Amaranta's little Fiat leave the forecourt of the winemaking co-operative.

★ ★ ★ ★ ★

The morning after he was just sitting about, doing nothing in particular. Given their late night, he did not expect Amaranta before the time she normally started preparing his lunch – he had in fact told her when she left that she should henceforth come and go as she liked. 'But you pay me, Leander!' she had protested. He had laughed. 'Don't be so formal. In fact, that's what at Pepalmar's somebody said I was. What I mean: we also agreed, didn't we, that you are the Lady of the Castle?' He had long realized, and he concluded again while looking into the morning sun and across to Alpiniano's Court from his study, that despite her enormous physical self-confidence she thrived on reassurance. Turning away from the open window, he went over to his desk. He suddenly felt a desire to reread his diary. The days since his return had been eventful – he wondered how easily he would be able to re-enter the spirit of his earlier Opaco and Fluentia impressions. Impressions which, after all, contained seeds of the evidence he hoped to provide the district attorney with. When he held the diary in his hands, he had another idea: this was the moment, he said to himself, to re-visit that great Gothic cathedral, built because in a nearby village the host had started bleeding during communion – and to find out how some scientists had recently tried to explain that miracle. He put his diary back into the desk. Shortly after, he heard Amaranta enter the house.

'Are you coming with me?' They were standing in the hall; he had told her where he was going, and why.

She was obviously surprised at his suggestion. After a moment, she started shaking her head. She would need more notice, she said; she could not just leave her son on his own. 'Mind you: since he became, so to speak, your first lieutenant here, he has started doing things in my own house which I would not have thought him capable of.' She looked at him, and then threw her arms around him. 'Leander, darling – I would have loved to! I have not been anywhere for ages. Thank you, anyway!'

She started kissing him. How neatly bodies fit each other, he thought – even though they were both dressed. It was of course all due to her agility: a former ballerina's, he mused fondly.

'I have a question before I leave,' he said.

'Which is?' She broke away from him, but still held his hand.

'You have always been very dismissive of Dupré; once, you even hinted that he was to blame for Cesini having strayed from the straight and narrow. What actually is the relationship between these two?'

As in earlier situations when he had broached a serious issue, her eyes became very big. 'To begin with, my father never liked Dupré; therefore I grew up feeling doubtful about him. And as to my ex: Cesini was the poor kid who grew up near the somewhat older and rich kid – Dupré. When Cesini was still a teenager, he saved Dupré from drowning. Dupré then paid for Cesini to attend art school. But at the time, Dupré had already started collecting paintings, sculptures and antiques. Like a maniac, in fact. Somebody nicknamed him The Hoover – it was said that he stopped at nothing. And as the poor kid had always admired the rich kid, Cesini eventually dropped out of art school and became one of The Hoover's accessories. I did not fully realize this for a long time. And as I said the other night: when I did, I threw Cesini out.'

★ ★ ★ ★ ★

Just as some twenty years previously, when he had commenced his studies in a nearby hilltop town and explored the surrounding countryside one weekend, the sight of Rotevio stunned Merten. Just as then, the rocky elevation on which the town was built had a reddish tinge: everything was bathed in sunlight. He stopped his car to take in the spectacle. Like Fonteluce, Rotevio had been one of the bastions of the country's most ancient culture – one of the last strongholds to surrender to the all-powerful emperors of a new age. And yet, he thought: after centuries of decline, when finally his northern ancestors the Goths became a menace to the south, this acropolis regained some of its earlier significance. Princes of the church sojourned here with their courts; and it was one of them who, fearing a siege, had commissioned the building of the most spectacular well Merten had ever seen.

His search, the reason for his visit to Rotevio, was to prove inconclusive. Immediately after he had booked into an hotel, he walked to the local museum. But the place was closed indefinitely – the closure, Merten learnt at a bar round the corner, was due to a lack of funds. The next day, he telephoned his at one time mentor: the professor who, at his first university, had awarded him the prize which at the time made him think there were no other goals worth a big effort. The professor had not heard of any attempt to explain the miracle of the bleeding host in the village near Rotevio. Had it just been a newspaper story, written by a sensation seeking hack? Or an attempt at catching the spotlight by a mediocre academic? Merten, who had chanced upon the story while first recuperating at Charlottenfels, decided it was either the one or the other. Hence, as the evening before, he walked over to and spent some time sitting outside the cathedral. What a magnificent structure! And what magnificent frescoes inside – these, painted by one of the foremost artists of the period, had soon after inspired a religious group of travelling players to perform episodes from the sermons of the Antichrist in the square in which he, Merten, was now sitting. Although that spectacle had for centuries been a mere memory, another one was not beyond his reach. Annually, on the day of Corpus Domini, the sacramental linen from the village church where the host had started bleeding during communion was carried in procession through the streets of Rotevio. He knew he would have to come back; and he also knew that, next time, he would endeavour not to come on his own.

On the morning of his departure, he visited the cathedral once more. He had always felt that although the artist responsible for the Last Judgement frescoes on the ceiling had not yet fully grasped the lessons of anatomy, his visions were more terrifying than those of some contemporaries whose reputation rested on their depiction of the Apocalypse. To be trapped, naked, in pools of ice! When Merten finally emerged into the square, the warm air of summer hit him. He walked aimlessly through the alleys and streets of the town for a while. Finally, he paused on a terrace which overlooked the plain to the south. He knew that like him, some seven hundred years before, a pope had looked down from here – to watch some boy of northern origin and his army on their march towards the Eternal City. The youth – blond, blue-eyed, only fifteen but nevertheless a duke in his own country – seemed unstoppable. Yet, the year after, the very same youth met a sticky end. When about an hour later Merten left Rotevio, he remembered how some fraud had postured as and tried to prolong the legend of that golden boy.

★ ★ ★ ★ ★

When he reached the southern suburbs of Fluentia, the heat had become unbearable. On the road, he had listened to the car radio – and according to the local station's weather bulletin, even the day before had been hotter than any day in the past few years. He remembered how at Fonteluce, when he was Pepalmar's neighbour, he used to do his downtown shopping early in the morning and return and seek shelter underneath the trees long before midday. Fluentia in summer could be like a cauldron. Especially today, he thought – and especially for those trapped in a car. From where he crossed the river, both the road to Opaco and the one to the historical centre were not far. As he needed a refreshing drink, and as parking was easy in the mid-afternoon hours, he drove into the centre.

The café was almost empty, and Berenice was not there. Although all the doors were open, there was no draught. Not even the electric ventilators underneath the ceiling were working; the barman, whom Merten asked what was wrong with them, just shrugged his shoulders. In fact, the staff in their black jackets all looked pitiable. Merten finished his drink quickly and cast a furtive glance in the direction of the Samira fresco. But however much he wanted to get out into the open air, he decided that for a loyal man this was not the way to leave – hence, he walked over to the corner underneath the fresco to pay tribute to the courtesan. Even though he knew now that the picture was a fake. What he saw made him forget that he was feeling uncomfortable. Was he imagining things? No – he looked harder and there was no doubt: the extremities of Samira's reddish hair looked wet. He remembered his Brionnac lesson. Had Cesini, to heighten the effect of his restoration, used a concoction which in a high temperature could liquefy? And if so: had the madonna wept blood again? He marched straight to the telephone booth and rang his villa.

When Amaranta answered, he felt that something was wrong. No, she said, the madonna had not wept. He knew that, situated in the hills like Fonteluce, Opaco was never quite as hot as Fluentia. 'Where are you, Leander?' she wanted to know. He told her, and she seemed to relax.

'Are you eager to see me, then?' he ventured.

'Yes – and not just for the obvious reason.' She paused. 'The villa was broken into last night.'

As he walked outside, he noticed that some new guests had arrived. He knew one of them. She was accompanied by a girl of about nine or ten.

'So this is the girl Silvana,' he said to the mother when he stood in front of them.

'Leander!' She got up and drew her daughter to her. 'This man has heard about *you*. And' – looking at Merten – 'this young lady has heard about *you*.'

The girl gave him a wonderful smile. She had her mother's eyes, he thought; her hair and her complexion were darker, though.

'But which one should I call Silvana now? And which one Sylvie?'

'Oh, she is Sylvie,' the mother said. I just loved confusing you for a moment, at Pepalmar's.'

He sat down with them. But he told them that he could not stay – that he had just learnt his villa had been broken into. He asked Silvana how she was; both in her chair and when she had got up she had struck him as very mobile, and he said so.

'Some days I am better. Today for instance. It always makes me hopeful, because the doctors say that I might yet recover – but they also say they have no way of telling for certain.'

The little girl, meanwhile, had studied him intently. 'I thought you were older,' she said in a matter-of-fact voice.

He laughed. 'But I am old. Very old,' he added confidentially.

'How old?' the child wanted to know.

'One day, I shall tell you, Sylvie; and it will then be a secret just between you and me.'

A merry laugh came from the mother. 'You haven't changed much, Leander. You still choose the right moment to charm your ladies.'

'But I am a serious man,' he protested.

Silvana looked at him thoughtfully. 'I know,' she said. 'Tell me: do you mind me ringing you at the villa? Pepalmar dropped a few comments about some shady art business you hoped to uncover. And now there is this burglary. Frankly, I find it worrying.'

No, of course he did not mind, he said. 'You have the number, anyway.' She too, he decided, had not changed much – he had always admired her discretion.

'Do tell me, Sylvie,' he asked as he was getting up, 'where did you leave your little brother?'

'He is far away,' the child replied, 'where I lived before we came to Fluentia. My grandparents are looking after him.'

'Don't you miss him?' She looked doubtful. 'To talk to, perhaps?' he suggested.

'Perhaps. But he is not interested in the things I want to talk about.'

Merten laughed and gave her a friendly wink. 'One day, he will be. And then I shall be even older – much too old for you to want to talk to me!'

When shortly after he was on the road to Opaco, he unsuccessfully tried to establish what impact Silvana's reappearance in his life was having on him. No doubt they would before long meet on their own – he wondered whether he would know then.

★ ★ ★ ★ ★

When he drove into the forecourt of the winemaking co-operative, he noticed the absence of Amaranta's little Fiat. Maybe she had driven over to her place and would be back for dinner. But as he walked up the steps to the villa, the main door stood open and he heard her move about in the kitchen. He called her name, and she came out into the hall. Whereas, at seeing her, he felt quite elated, she was very serious; and when they embraced, he realized that she had been frightened.

'So tell me all about this break-in,' he said, drawing her into the lounge and onto the sofa. 'I see no damage, by the way.'

She pointed to the window: 'This was smashed – but I already had the glazier in to fit new panes.'

Once again, her eyes became very big, and she pressed his hand as if to reassure herself that he was there. 'It was terrible, Leander – I was in the house when it happened!'

He was astounded. 'How come?'

She told him that, in the morning of the previous day, there had been something wrong with her car. She called the mechanic, who collected the vehicle and said he would bring it back once it was repaired.

'I did actually wonder why it is not outside,' Merten remarked with a smile. 'But why were you here at night?'

'Due to the car problem I was not able to do as much work as usual – and suddenly, I noticed that it was getting late. I telephoned Davide, who said he was fine on his own.' She looked at Merten and relaxed a little. 'I said to myself' – now she also smiled – 'that it would be quite nice to keep your bed warm for you. And that's what I did.' He admitted her decision appealed to him. 'But it was very hot, and I could not sleep. To let in fresh air, I had left a couple of doors and windows in the upstairs rooms open. And suddenly, there was this sound of breaking glass coming from downstairs. Followed by steps.' She paused, and he stroked her gently. 'I was terrified when I heard the intruder come up the stairs. And even more so when he was in your study; he used a torch, and through the half-open door I saw its beam of light glide along your shelves and drawers. Even if I had wanted to, I could not have stirred – I felt paralysed, lying in your bed all the while. Then there was a noise from the forecourt of the co-operative, made by two or three people returning late. The intruder left immediately; and when I had regained my composure I telephoned Gastone, who shortly after came over with two of his men.'

What a scary experience, Merten thought; and how easily it could have ended badly for her!

'But this isn't all, Leander. The man – I am pretty sure it was only one person – left through the main door! I heard him open and lock it again. My keys to the villa were up here with me. It's a habit – since at home I have a front door which is partly of glass, I never leave the keys inside.' She paused. 'It means the intruder had a key. Which he only used when he was disturbed and in a hurry to leave. He knew of course that, as he had smashed a window, the whole thing would be seen as a standard burglary by whoever was going to investigate '.

A little later, he went up to the study. Amaranta said she had not cleared all the mess, because she guessed that he wanted some of the things scattered over the floor in a particular drawer or order. He wondered why she had never re-married; she would make a great wife for any man in favour of wedlock. As he looked around the room, he had the strange feeling that nothing was missing. All the pictures were there – even the few he had acquired since his return to Fluentia – and also the group of small wooden sculptures which, like the rest, belonged to the villa. So what had the intruder come for? Money? Merten never kept much money at home. And whatever he kept was usually somewhere in the bedroom. The loss of it would not bother him – although the mere thought that, if undisturbed, the burglar could have gone in there did.

Whilst he was picking up things and putting them back into their accustomed place, he tried to work out the logic behind the break-in. The circumstances were quite plain, really. To begin with, whoever was behind the whole thing must have noticed that his car was not around. And had he not, it suddenly occurred to him, also told Dupré at Berenice's that he was thinking of going away again? From the window, he looked across to Alpiniano's Court. Secondly, he concluded that whoever watched from there – or even just from the main road – would not, once Amaranta had withdrawn to the bedroom, have seen a light. Not even if, once she had gone to bed, she did not switch off the light instantly. The bedroom and the study were on opposite sides of the villa. Thirdly: the absence of Amaranta's car would have been noticed – which made the intruder believe, wrongly, that she too was not in. But what had the burglar come for? Merten heard Amaranta's steps on the stairs, and as she entered the study he turned round.

'Did you tell Gastone about the intruder having a key to the main door?'

'Not when Gastone first came, because he had these two men with him. But, yes, this morning I did.' Merten still stood in the window, and she sat down at his desk, facing him. 'We were discussing it in the garden when this awful man the marshal arrived – who, unfortunately, heard most of what I said. But I guess I would have had to tell him anyway?'

Merten nodded. 'I guess so – unless you did not want to do the correct thing.' He smiled encouragingly. 'And what did this paragon of intelligence and integrity, the marshal, have to say?'

'Oh, he dismissed my observations as mere fantasy. In fact, Gastone and the marshal disagreed sharply, and there was quite an argument between them. In the end, he started questioning us about you. Gastone cut him short – he told him that if he wanted to know anything about you, he could come and ask you personally.'

Merten was rather amused. 'Quite right,' he said. 'I look forward immensely to receiving this big buffoon.'

She looked at him questioningly, and he walked over to his desk to give her a kiss. She has not yet discovered my darker sides, he said to himself. He knew that these had to do with the fact that he was born and brought up in volcano country.

★ ★ ★ ★ ★

For the first time, Amaranta had spent the night with him. It was she who had proposed it; she needed, in her own words, to ban the recent memories of her solitary stay in the villa – memories both acoustic and visual – from her mind. 'What about Davide?' he had asked. 'Oh, Davide is fine. He has, to my surprise, even started mixing with people of his own age. You know, they gather in the squares of the villages in the evening.'

A surprise indeed, Merten thought, when the morning after he stood under the shower. Then he pondered over another question of his – what about the threat of burglars to her place? There was none, according to her. 'Mind you,' she had added, perhaps because he had indicated agreement, 'I am not living in a hovel. I do have a nice house – and I want you to visit me there soon! Anyway: it has always been a fervent wish of Davide's to be there in the event of a burglary. It is probably the only thing he has always had – let's say: before you employed him – a clear scenario for.' In his shower cubicle, Merten thought of the lad's impressive build and decided there was no need to worry. At this moment, the telephone rang.

Amaranta came up the stairs and into the bathroom: it was the district attorney, she said. Merten put on a gown and answered the call from his study.

Talon sounded very amicable – he had no news but he had enjoyed their meeting. Besides, they had a mutual friend: Pepalmar. He too had been invited to the professor's recent reception – 'but I did not know of your relations with him until the morning of the event, when I had to ring and say I was unexpectedly prevented from attending.' All the more reason for the two of them to meet socially, the attorney added – 'Hence, I wondered whether you would care to have lunch with me one day?' Merten said he would be delighted – and they agreed to meet on the very day.

Two hours later, just before he left for Fluentia, Merten popped in on Gastone. The moment he saw Merten, the steward looked worried. 'I really only have an inkling of your professional activities and interests, sir,' he said after they had exchanged a few words about the break-in; 'but if I knew more – I hope you won't mind me saying so – I would probably be able to put my finger on what's behind this whole thing.' They agreed that in a day or two, they would have lunch together in the villa and have a good talk.

Although the temperature had not changed much – perhaps it was slightly less hot than the day before – Merten went to the café before proceeding to the restaurant the district attorney had suggested. He asked for a glass of sparkling wine, waved to Berenice, who was busy at the till, and walked straight over to the corner underneath the Samira fresco. The courtesan's hair was the same as the day before: the extremities looked wet. A few more degrees, he thought, and the paint would start trickling down. From the corner of his eye, he saw that Berenice had left her seat and was coming over to him.

She cast a brief glance at the ceiling and shook her head teasingly: 'Why can't you ever leave the ladies alone, Leander?'

He kissed her on the cheek. 'Have you seen this?' he asked.

'Seen what?'

He lowered his voice and told her. She was fascinated.

'May I ask you a favour, *madame*?'

She laughed. 'You know you always may, *Dr. Merten.*'

He would be obliged, he said, if she did not discuss his observations with anyone. 'Except Dupré,' he added – 'but don't tell him I said so. You may tell him, though, that I was the one who noticed the change.'

She nodded spontaneously. He had to hand it to her, he thought: she had a quick mind, and her smile could be sublime.

'You may count on me,' she said; 'although it drives me mad that I don't know what is going on in your mind!'

He gave her hand a friendly squeeze. One day she would know, he promised.

The district attorney waited in the reception area of the restaurant. 'I am Constantin,' he said when they shook hands.

'Leander,' Merten replied.

Shortly after, during lunch, he told his host as concisely as possible what he had witnessed in the café years ago, what he had seen and heard at Chandio, what he knew about Dupré and his associates at Opaco and what – due to the heat, no doubt – was happening in the café right now.

The attorney had not interrupted him once; at the end, having looked almost incredulous at times, he leaned back and laughed good-naturedly. 'It had never crossed my mind that I would get something out of this lunch, Leander. Anyway, district attorneys are not into this kind of entertainment – maybe I should write a manual for members of my profession?'

Again, Merten felt there was an affinity between them. 'So what's your verdict, Constantin?'

Talon said he would instruct the men from the bureau of criminal investigation to watch the weeping madonna as if they were hell-hounds. 'Let's hope it gets hotter, Leander – and then we will have a celebratory lunch in the village above Opaco.'

Merten finally mentioned the break-in, and also what he had just said to Berenice.

The attorney looked thoughtful. 'Obviously,' he then said, 'you don't know whether these guys at Opaco have an idea of you knowing something. And by making your observations in the café available to them, you have now set a trap. Congratulations. I shall make sure the boys from the bureau will keep an eye on your villa.'

Merten said he was most grateful, and there was a pause between them.

'May I be indiscreet and ask who the lady is who answers your telephone?' the attorney ventured.

'She is my housekeeper,' Merten replied. 'More precisely: I also have a relationship with her. Please feel free to tell or ask her anything – her name is Amaranta.'

The attorney nodded approvingly. 'It is a name given, when you and I were children, to a girl by parents who believed she was born to be loved.' He raised his glass: 'To the health of Leander and Amaranta. The lady's voice makes me believe that you are a very lucky man.'

★ ★ ★ ★ ★

The morning after, he was still having his breakfast when somebody rang the doorbell. Amaranta had gone up to the village to do the shopping; hence, he rose from the table to see who the caller was. It was the marshal.

'I believe you are Merten,' the man said after a moment, having looked him up and down quite insolently.

'Dr. Merten to you,' was the icy reply.

Whilst the marshal was working on a new approach, Merten, who had stepped outside, closed the door behind him – he was not going to let this fellow enter the villa.

'Well … sir,' the voice of authority finally said, 'I thought I'd better let you know that, as far as this break-in goes, there is nothing to worry about. There are gypsies in the area, and I am sure it was them. They normally look for money, jewellery or any valuables which can be sold quickly – and I have no doubt that you are covered by insurance. May I ask if you have noticed anything missing?'

Merten said he had not.

'Good,' the marshal said, puffing himself up. He seemed to feel reinstated in his role. Merten wondered what was coming.

After a few casual comments on the villa and its immediate surroundings, the marshal cleared his voice. 'It has come to my attention,' he said, 'that you take an interest in …' – his hand vaguely indicated the hillside above Opaco – '… in the wonderful events which, recently, have made the village up there famous.'

No doubt, Merten thought, the man knew of his talks with the sacristan and Dupré – and also that he had bought one of Cesini's statues. He might even have heard of his two visits to the village. But had Dupré been to the café since his talk with Berenice the day before – and if so, could the news have prompted the marshal to come and see him? He encouraged the man with the faintest of smiles – he was not going to make it easy for him.

The marshal thrust out his chest and attempted a sharp glance. 'Perhaps I should say to you,' he said, 'that the locals here do not, as a rule, take kindly to newcomers who are being too inquisitive. In fact,' he added after a moment, misreading Merten's silence, 'some such newcomers, I mean people of an overtly curious disposition, soon realized that life elsewhere suited them much better.'

Merten felt that one of those rare moments when he lost his temper was imminent – moments which, because they were rare, were legendary. He also knew that he was going to be very cruel to the marshal.

'Are you suggesting,' he said mildly, 'that I might be well advised not to make efforts to prolong my stay here?' Before the marshal could reply, Merten confided to him that he had once, in a far away country, been in a similar situation. 'Two men came to see me in my apartment. They wore bulging jackets and told me that they belonged to a certain powerful organisation – "We would like you to leave", they said without much ceremony.'

The marshal listened avidly. 'And did you leave?'

'Yes,' Merten said; 'within fifteen minutes. And I never visited the country again.' The marshal nodded approvingly. 'I instantly went to pack my suitcase,' Merten continued, 'and then I telephoned the ambulance.'

'The ambulance?' The marshal looked nonplussed.

Again, Merten answered in the affirmative. 'When I had packed,' he said, 'I took two long steps across those two men, who were lying on the floor in front of me, closed the door and hailed a taxi to the airport. They were big men, by the way,' he added, stepping up to the marshal, who was turning pale. 'Don't ever come here again to issue veiled threats to me,' he said coldly. 'You know, you could have an accident – just look at those steep stone steps going down right behind you.'

He was about to turn to the door when his temper finally erupted. 'Just get out of my sight, you bloody idiot!' he shouted at the marshal, who instinctively grabbed hold of the stair-rail.

As he slammed the door behind him, he knew he had made an enemy for life. He did not care. Peace at all cost had never, since his adolescent years, interested him – he had always preferred creeps, opportunists and manipulators to know what he thought of them. For a little while, he paced up and down aimlessly; he would have to telephone Talon and tell him of this visit, he thought. The moment he intended to do so, he heard Amaranta on the steps. As he was still in the hall, he opened the door for her.

'What have you done to that marshal, Leander?' She looked startled and amused at the same time. 'I bumped into him in the forecourt, and he struck me as absolutely shell-shocked.'

Merten laughed; then he looked at her shopping bags. 'Is there anything in these bags which cannot be kept until tomorrow?'

She shook her head. 'Why?'

He stroked her bare arms and finally rested his hands on her hips. 'You look splendid,' he said – 'I want to take you out for lunch. There is this little castle in the hills beyond Fonteluce – it used to be a toll station in the late Middle Ages. Have you eaten there before?' She said that she had not, but that she knew of the place. 'Let's go there,' he announced. Her obvious delight at the suggestion made her look most bewitching, he thought. He added that he would tell her over lunch of his adventure with the local hero the marshal.

'You look mischievous, Leander,' she said with a questioning smile.

'I was,' he answered. He consulted his watch. 'Shall we go in about an hour? I would like to read something before.' All of a sudden, he had decided that this was the right moment to peruse his diary again.

Leaving in an hour was fine with her, she said; and while she took the shopping bags through to the kitchen, he went upstairs and into his study. He opened the right bottom drawer of the desk and removed some newspaper articles and a notepad which he had deliberately put on top of the diary. When his hand touched the bottom of the drawer, he realized that the diary was missing.

★ ★ ★ ★ ★

Although he had discussed the theft of the diary with Amaranta, their outing, followed by an amorous late afternoon at the villa, had made him take this latest discovery rather lightly. The morning after, however, he woke up in the early hours and was unable to go to sleep again. What would the thief – or the people behind him – be able to infer from his entries? He got up long before Amaranta was due, made himself breakfast and afterwards went up to his study. From the window, he looked across to Alpiniano's Court – once more, just as on his journey back from Brionnac, he tried to rehearse the diary from memory.

He had been sitting at the desk for a while when he heard the heavy main door open and close. As he was often in his study when Amaranta arrived – even if he rose at his usual time rather than at dawn – he knew she would before long come upstairs. Especially as in the kitchen she would see that he had already had breakfast. He got up to turn on the radio, but realized he had missed the news he always listened to; and as he did not like the modern composer whose music was being played, he switched the set off again. When he turned round, there was a knock on the door. Then there was another. He wondered what made her knock twice.

'Yes?'

The door opened, and Davide stood in the frame. 'May I come in?'

'Of course you may.' Merten laughed; 'excuse my surprise, but I did not expect you.'

'I know.' It struck him then that the lad looked very serious rather than, as usual, just reserved. 'There has been a bad accident down on the Opaco road,' he finally said.

Merten felt a cold hand reach out towards him. He groped for his library chair and motioned Davide to sit down on the sofa underneath the bookshelves.

'My mother is still down there, talking to the marshal and his deputies,' he heard the boy say – 'but she is very upset, and as I am working here today, I decided to come and tell you.'

Merten was still stunned, but also amazed – what an excellent lad, he thought.

'So who was involved in this accident?' he asked.

'Gastone,' Davide said after a pause. There was another pause. 'He is dead.'

'I can't believe it!' Merten thought of the meal and talk he was going to have with the steward. 'And whose was the other car?'

Davide shook his head. There was no other car, he said. Apparently, Gastone had just lost control in one of the bends – his car, which had probably turned over several times, was found near the river that ran some ninety feet underneath the road.

'Lost control?' Merten, who remembered how skilfully Gastone took those bends on their drive back from the airport, shook his head.

'Well,' the boy said, 'that's the marshal's view.'

Of course, Merten thought. 'The marshal, Davide, is an idiot!'

The lad could not help a quick, conspiratorial grin. 'There are some people here who would agree with you,' he ventured.

'Gastone did,' Merten countered. 'Was he dead when the vehicle was discovered down by the river?'

Davide nodded. 'They found him with his neck broken.'

When Amaranta came in, Merten took her down to the garden and sat with her for a while.

She cried. 'I knew him since I was a little girl – he used to come to the bar which, at the time, my father owned up there.' She looked wistfully in the direction of the village on the hillside.

As she got up, saying it was time she went over to the house, her eyes were again full of tears. Knowing that it would please her, Merten praised the manly way Davide had handled the bad news; he also said that, as they had talked, he noticed that her son, with his new haircut, was beginning to change into a rather smart young fellow. As he had expected, she began to brighten up.

'What a day for him!' he said.

'Yes,' she replied quietly – 'especially as it is his birthday.'

It was her son's nineteenth. After Amaranta had gone into the villa, Merten looked out for Davide from the steps. When he saw him at the bottom of the garden, he called and motioned him to come up. At the same time, he descended the steps and took his bicycle out of the storeroom underneath.

'Happy birthday,' he said – 'Amaranta just told me. Would you like this machine as a present?'

If ever there was somebody who did not expect anything, he thought, it was Davide.

'But don't you need it to exercise yourself?' the boy asked, incredulous.

'No longer, really. I was quite strong before my operation; although' – Merten smiled – 'perhaps not quite as strong as you are. Anyway, I am in fine form again, which is basically due to how your wonderful mother looks after me.' He held out his hand. 'Once more: happy birthday! This machine is yours.'

The boy looked overwhelmed. He shook Merten's hand. Merten invited him to go for a ride. But Davide did not move. 'I am glad my mother met you,' he said in his genuine, somewhat old-fashioned way. Again Merten, who was touched, remembered the dignified manners of the boy's grandfather.

★ ★ ★ ★ ★

The days leading up to Gastone's funeral were very quiet. Amaranta said that in the winemaking co-operative the mood was at a low as well. The steward was going to be buried in his native village, on the plains near the sea. Merten felt pleased when he heard it; his final resting place, he thought, would suit Gastone. There, his spirit would be reunited with the spirit of fiery horses and generations of daring riders, past and present – the only constant music being the sounds of the tide coming in and going out, and the drumming of hooves on the dunes along the beach.

In the early morning of the day before the funeral, Amaranta had gone down to Fluentia to buy herself a suitable dress. Even in the hills, it had become unbearably hot. When she came back, they agreed that in the evening Merten would go over to her place for dinner.

'It's about time, Leander,' she said with a reproachful smile as they were having a bite at lunchtime.

Due to the heat, and perhaps the impending event, neither of them was hungry. She went home in the early afternoon, and as he looked across to Alpiniano's Court from his study, it occurred to him that – depending on who had the diary – Amaranta could be at risk. He had told the district attorney of his encounter with the marshal, and also that he could not endorse the latter's verdict on what caused Gastone's fatal accident; but he now thought it was a good idea to ring Talon again. And it was probably an equally good idea to pay a visit to Pepalmar. The professor had a large collection of firearms, and even the ancient ones were mostly in working order – no doubt, Merten thought, his friend would lend him a gun.

Later in the afternoon, just as he was going to telephone Pepalmar, the district attorney rang.

'Have you heard that the madonna wept again, Leander?'

'No!' Merten was surprised, admitting that in the last few days miracles had been rather far from his mind.

'Anyway,' the attorney continued, 'I had the statue confiscated instantly – it is right now being re-examined at Fluentia University. And I have also sent one of my men over to your café to look at the fresco. I have a feeling we shall soon make progress.' Talon sounded very confident. 'By the way,' he added, 'I have delayed the steward's funeral.'

'Why?' Merten, taken aback, said that he had planned to attend it.

'The coroner says that there is something which puzzles him about the dead man's neck. I had of course told him that you dismiss the marshal's interpretation of the accident.'

Before he went over to her for dinner, Merten rang Amaranta to say that the funeral was off. After he arrived at her place, she told him that Davide had asked her to excuse him.

'Since you gave him your bike, I have hardly seen him. One might say' – she laughed – 'that you have alienated him from me.'

She took him on a tour through the house, and Merten was quite impressed. The building was old and of a rural aspect – he could see that her and her father's means had been limited, but that nevertheless they had lavished a lot of care on their home.

Whilst they sat at dinner he told her that, since like Gastone she was mentioned in the diary, he was worried on her behalf.

'May I know,' she inquired with a playful smile, 'what you wrote about me, *Dr. Merten?*'

'I can't tell you word for word. But whoever reads the diary must conclude that I fancied you. Besides, there are references to our talks about Cesini and Dupré.'

She had laughed after his first admission, but then turned serious. 'Don't worry. If Dupré is behind the weeping madonna and the theft of the diary – just as he is no doubt behind that fraudulent fresco business – Cesini as his henchman would not tolerate somebody raising a hand against me … although he has undoubtedly heard about you and me. People living near the villa have seen more than you think, dear Leander.' She went quiet and looked thoughtful. 'God knows whether it was Cesini who broke into the villa; but if it was,' she concluded, 'he did not know that I was there.'

Not for the first time, Merten pondered on the hold Amaranta seemed to have on Cesini. And on how she managed to turn men's heads. After all, here he was himself, more than a decade after his crazy Strange Fruit days. As he looked at her, he remembered the bonfire and her dance on St. John's Eve.

Back in the villa, he telephoned Pepalmar and asked if he could visit him the day after. Any time, the professor said. Just when he was about to go to bed, the district attorney called again.

'Constantin – you keep surprising me!'

The attorney apologised for the late hour. 'But' – he said – 'the blood on the madonna's face is not blood! And I have more news. The boys from the central bureau of investigation have once more interrogated the villager who is the owner of the statue. Apparently, the man is about to crack up – he has told them that a local artist friend had repaired the statue. Mark you: when it still stood in the villager's garden, and before it wept for the first time! And who was that artist friend? The name is Cesini.' Talon paused for effect. 'I have also had news about the fresco in the café. Your courtesan's hair is dripping!'

Merten wondered whether he still needed a gun. He guessed what was coming next: Talon said that in the morning he was going to issue a warrant for Cesini's arrest.

'Maybe you could put out your feelers and contact that old notary at Rabussin – please ask him, if you don't mind, whether he would be willing to come to Fluentia for purposes of identification. Because once I have Cesini,' Talon added, 'I shall probably want to arrest the sacristan as well.' Merten said he had not seen the sacristan for ages. 'Don't worry,' the attorney replied, 'we will get him.'

On the day Gastone should have been buried, Merten drove out to Pepalmar's place. He told the professor as much as he could, without being tedious, about what he had become involved in. Again, as many times before, he was glad that

Pepalmar did not need long-winded explanations. They went upstairs to the room with the firearms collection.

'You won't panic, will you?' Pepalmar asked, offering him a revolver he said was one of his most treasured possessions.

Merten laughed. 'My father would have told you that for the son of a distinguished military man, panic is not even supposed to be part of the vocabulary.'

When they were downstairs again, just before Merten left, Pepalmar broached the subject of La Fandango. 'What about you and her?' he asked – 'I don't think,' he added as his visitor did not answer instantly, 'that her feelings for you have changed.'

'Perhaps mine for her have,' Merten said slowly. But he admitted he was not sure. It had occurred to him before that, when outside the café they last met, she indicated that she would ring him at the villa. Why had she not done so?

It was growing dusky when he returned to Opaco, and he was surprised to find Amaranta still in the villa. She was unusually monosyllabic. He went into the lounge to pour himself a drink and she followed him; it was quite clear that she was not doing anything in particular, but the longer he watched her from his easy-chair, the more he noticed how disconcerted she looked. Finally – she had started to close the shutters – he asked her what was wrong. She turned round, and her eyes were very big.

'Why didn't you tell me that you are a family man, Leander?'

'A what?' he asked, incredulous.

'Your wife and your daughter were here today.'

'Wonderful,' he said with a laugh; 'could you please tell me when – and where – I acquired them?'

She seemed close to tears and he got up to take her in his arms, but she drew back. 'Please don't joke,' she said; 'I thought both Silvana and the girl were adorable, but I would have preferred to know.'

Unprepared for the news of such a visit, he sat down again, this time on the sofa. But he could not help being amused by her conclusion.

'Silvana can't possibly have said she was my wife!' He turned serious. 'I was her lover, yes, but that was long ago. The relationship ended before I even saw you for the first time, down in Fluentia at the café. You may work out yourself how long ago this was. And although I thought of her at times, I knew next to nothing about her since her departure. When I arrived at Opaco, I did not even know she was back in this country; I met her almost accidentally at Pepalmar's, a couple of weeks ago.'

Amaranta seemed to relax – she had to see that he was telling the truth. He got up again and took her hand.

'She didn't say she was your wife ...'

'See!' he said reassuringly, drawing her onto to the sofa with him.

'But ...'

'But what?'

Amaranta looked at him. 'How often have you seen the little girl?'

'Just once. Last week – again, by accident.'

Amaranta still looked at him. 'She is the very picture of you! Apart from her eyes.'

Slowly, the message registered. This time he was glad he was sitting.

It was very late when Amaranta left. He urged her to stay, but she declined – although tenderly. A man as independent as he was, she said, needed time to himself to come to terms with fatherhood. 'Especially as the news has reached you so late. And indirectly.' She had not only regained her composure: he could now even read some slight amusement in her eyes. Her kiss was passionate – and he took in every movement of hers as she walked down the steps and disappeared into the night.

★ ★ ★ ★ ★

In the morning, when she came in, Amaranta had more news.

'Cesini was arrested yesterday!'

Since he had returned late, it had of course not struck Merten as strange that the stall down by the road was empty.

'I wonder,' she added, 'whether this has anything to do with the latest tests carried out on the madonna?'

'I am sure it has,' Merten said, remembering at the same time that he had not yet contacted the old notary at Rabussin. He told her he was going to make a couple of telephone calls. 'No doubt you shall soon know more.' He smiled. 'This time – for a change – I'll be the one with the news.'

He called the notary from his study, and the old man said he would happily oblige the district attorney – he had never been to Fluentia, but had always wanted to visit; hence, this would be an opportunity.

Merten then telephoned the attorney. 'The notary is at your disposal, Constantin,' he announced.

'Excellent!' Talon, who took it for granted that he knew of the arrest, told Merten they had made it quite obvious to Cesini that they had not just apprehended him in connection with the madonna. 'A certain fresco and a certain château were

163

mentioned to him *en passant*, and also that we hope to soon make the acquaintance of a certain sacristan. Cesini seemed quite shaken. Clearly, he and his friends at Opaco have no idea that you and I know each other. Be careful, Leander! As that lot up there are unaware of us having met, they may just want to prevent you from speaking to me.'

Merten told the attorney not to worry – he said he was on his guard.

'By the way,' Talon added, 'we don't know more than you re the sacristan's whereabouts. But we don't want to make too many noises at present. Especially as' – he laughed – 'your favourite the marshal must be all ears.'

When he thought about what he had just learnt, Merten concluded that, with Cesini in jail, Amaranta would very likely be in danger now. Unlike Cesini, Dupré was probably without scruples as far as she was concerned. He still believed that Gastone's death was no accident – and apart from the steward, his only constant source of information mentioned in the missing diary was Amaranta. As he rose to go and speak to her, he heard her on the stairs. He went over to the window instead; and as she walked though the open door, she came right up to him, putting her hands on his shoulders.

'Have you spoken to Silvana?' The question was unexpected.

'No,' he laughed, 'but she is next.'

He drew her closer to him and said he was again worried about her. Although, when he told her why, she shrugged the whole thing off, he insisted that for the time being she moved in with him. Did she have any problem with this?

'Not if you mean Davide; he is all right. Which means: no. It's fine with me.'

He mentioned that the place was big enough for Davide too — provided her son felt like coming with her. Amaranta said she would put it to him; but that, apart from joining them for meals, he would probably want to stay at home.

They agreed that she would move some of her things to the villa the day after. As they talked, her eyes alighted on the open top drawer of his desk. The gun was lying there. She started at the sight.

'Do you know how to handle these things, Leander?'

He responded with a dry chuckle. 'You are asking the son of a lieutenant-colonel — who himself was the son of a major-general. They both served in the artillery. When I was a boy at Charlottenfells, my father used to take me to the shooting gallery of a famous local arms factory. Due to the noise from the nearby waterfalls, you could hardly hear the incessant gunfire. Anyway: already at the age of thirteen, I was the better shot than the old man. Does that put your mind at ease, my lady?'

She smiled. 'How could I be unimpressed. I have waited all my life for a knight in shining armour!' There was a pause, and then she was in dead earnest. 'Please beware of that coachman, should you go near Dupré again.'

'Coachman? Who is he?'

'He runs a one-man enterprise as a carrier, and he also does funerals and weddings in this area. It is rumoured that he is also in Dupré's employment; and he has been over there — she pointed towards Alpiniano's Court though the open window — quite often of late.' Again, she paused. 'He is supposed to be the strongest man around here — I heard that he boasts he can break bones as easily as other men chop firewood. People's arms, for instance.'

Merten had heard enough. 'Or shall we say necks?' he asked. He thought of Gastone and of the fact that the coroner had delayed the steward's funeral.

After a little while, Amaranta went downstairs again. He asked her to leave the door open. Before he closed the top drawer of his desk, he took out his address book – then he rang Silvana.

'I was told you came here with my daughter,' he said when she answered.

'I beg your pardon?'

He repeated himself. She was silent for a moment.

'How do you know?' she finally asked – 'I mean: about you and Sylvie.'

He told her that Amaranta had been struck by their likeness. Again, she was silent.

'Why,' he wanted to know, 'didn't you tell me all those years ago, when you wrote to me after your departure from Fluentia?'

'I thought about it for a long time when I discovered that I was pregnant.' She paused. 'I can see now that I hesitated at first as I was hurt because you had made no effort to make me stay on in Fluentia. Anyway, I then started thinking about you. I had always known that professionally you would not go on doing what you were at the time, that your ultimate calling would be the pursuits of the mind. And I felt that if I owned up, and if because of this you compromised, you might be resentful one day.' That was the end of the story, she said.

'But what about your marriage?'

'Oh, yes,' she said: 'You may remember that in our Fluentia days I told you of the man – the son of a neighbouring landowner – my parents had lined up for me. Well, he is the one I married. He didn't mind about Sylvie – he was in fact rather good with her. And by marrying me, he of course turned me into a decent woman. As you did know before you met me again: the marriage didn't last.'

This time, Merten had gone silent. Finally, he asked her whether she had come to Opaco to tell him about the girl.

'No,' she said; 'I did intend to tell you before long – but I first had to see the lady you told me you had a relationship with.'

'And?' he wanted to know.

Her answer, like their meeting at Pepalmar's, floored him. 'With me, dearest Leander, you would be a man with a past. With the entrancing Amaranta, you are a man with a future.'

Indeed, he thought after their conversation: he needed time to himself. He went for a walk in the garden. He had ended by saying that he soon wanted to see Sylvie again. Silvana had said that the feeling was mutual – that the girl had greatly taken to him. 'Small wonder,' she had laughed, 'given your performance outside the café. Perhaps, as she is your daughter, you may consider a slightly different approach next time!'

He was still contemplating how to deal with the situation when Amaranta appeared in the entrance to the villa. She motioned him to come nearer.

'Dupré is on the phone,' she said as he walked up the steps. Her face told him that she had heard at least part of his conversation with Silvana. She stopped him before he could get to the telephone. 'He wants to see you at his place,' she whispered – 'don't go!'

When Merten spoke to him, Dupré was very smooth. In spite of some pleasant earlier meetings, they had not met for quite a while, the landlord said – would a drink at his place, around lunchtime the day after, be acceptable? Merten the chess-player had anticipated the move. He thanked Dupré; yes, he said, he would gladly be there at noon.

★ ★ ★ ★ ★

The day after, shortly before he was due at Dupré's, he sat in his study. There was a knock on the door. Then another. Again, after the first knock, he had thought it was Amaranta – and before he could react, the door opened and Davide walked in.

'I just wanted to say, Leander, that I am coming with you' – the window stood open, and with a movement of his head the lad indicated Alpiniano's Court.

'No, you are not!' As soon as he had said it, Merten regretted his brusque reply. Both the familiarity – the boy had never before addressed him by his name or anything – and the gesture moved him.

'Yes, I am' – Davide stood his ground.

Merten got up and put an arm round the lad's shoulders. 'Thank you,' he said – 'but may I suggest a different plan to you? I want to get some important information out of Dupré; and if I appeared with you as my bodyguard, he would be alarmed. So please let me deal with this on my own. However' – he stepped back to his desk to take a pen and paper – 'if I am not back within an hour and a half, do ring this number. The man who will answer is a Mr. Talon – he is the district attorney. Just tell him where I went; and that I didn't come back.'

Davide's eyes lit up – it was obvious to Merten that he had got the right measure of the boy.

Almost immediately after Davide, he walked down the stairs as well. The gun was in one of the pockets of his jacket. When he reached the bottom of the stairs, the formidable shape of

Amaranta blocked his path. She was dressed more seductively than ever.

'There is no way out,' she announced; 'I want you here, with me.'

'I'll be back,' he promised, pushing her aside very gently – 'and I shall remind you of what you just said.'

In another attempt to hold him back, she gripped his wrist. 'Can't you hear the dogs, barking incessantly in the woods over there? It's a bad omen.' He was surprised at how terrified she looked. 'Darling Leander, one fatal accident has been enough!'

Again, he freed himself gently. 'I quite agree with you. And somebody over there is going to pay for that accident.'

★ ★ ★ ★ ★

9

Alpiniano's Cave

When he walked across the main road and up to the little church, the barking got louder. In front of Dupré's house, the shady grove with its earthen mounds once more made him wonder about the mysterious Alpiniano and his seat. After he had looked about himself for a moment, he walked up to the house. He rang the bell, noticing at the same time that the front door stood ajar. There was no reply, and he rang again. Finally he knocked, then pushed the door open and entered. As there was nobody to be seen, he walked through the lobby and into the lounge, where he had had his previous drink with Dupré. He had been careful not to close the front door behind him. The lounge too looked deserted. But didn't he hear music from somewhere? Indeed – in the corner where the house was built against the church, he noticed another open door. It was very narrow. As he approached it, the music seemed to have come nearer. A spiral staircase, which was illuminated, led to some lower area. He suspected it was the undercroft of the church and started to descend slowly.

His guess was right. As he reached the bottom of the stairs and walked though yet another door, he found himself in a huge, vaulted crypt. What he saw beggared belief. The place was crammed with works of art. Dupré's collection! As the thought flashed across his mind, he was seized roughly from behind and his arms were held in a vice-like grip.

'Don't try anything silly, my friend,' a voice hissed in his ear.

Merten was furious. Not with the fellow behind him, but with himself – like an idiot, he had walked into a trap.

'Nice to meet you,' he said to his new acquaintance, turning his head as far as he could. Both the size and the strength of the fellow made him realize that he owed his welcome to the coachman Amaranta had warned him against.

He was trying to ascertain if the coachman was the only person standing behind him when he noticed a movement in the farthest corner of the crypt. A man in richly embroidered clothes walked towards a pulpit – Merten decided that even this rather imposing structure had not originally stood there, but was part of the collection which surrounded him. The man went up into the pulpit, and Merten recognized Dupré. There was another movement in the distant corner, and two more people appeared: the sacristan and the marshal. None of them took much notice of the visitor; perhaps, Merten thought, they were waiting for a sign from their chief. But Dupré seemed totally oblivious to everybody around him. He looked as if he was studying some papers.

Turning his head again, Merten asked the coachman whether he thought they were going to be treated to a sermon. The fellow snarled and tightened his grip.

'Let go of him!' Dupré had finally looked up, and his voice was quite sharp.

The coachman only complied with one hand – which he used to check Merten's pockets. 'He's got a gun!'

Suddenly, everyone's eyes were on Merten. 'Be careful not to hurt yourself,' Merten warned as the coachman disarmed him. He felt that by verbally provoking his Herculean adversary he might somehow gain the upper hand. But before the coachman could react, Dupré addressed his visitor.

'Dr. Merten, you surprise me – I don't think any guest of mine has ever felt a need to carry a firearm on him.' Dupré turned to the coachman. 'As I said: let go of him. And give that gun to the marshal. Let's do things properly at Alpiniano's Court.'

As the gun changed hands, Dupré once more seemed to have forgotten the company assembled before him. This time, his eyes travelled adoringly over the treasures which filled the crypt. The solemn music, wherever it came from, was still playing. Merten, who was intrigued by a picture on the wall behind the pulpit, made a tentative step forward. Instantly, both the coachman and the marshal moved towards him.

'Easy, boys,' he said, 'easy! I'm interested in the art here.' He turned to Dupré, who had again looked up. 'I must say I do take exception to your pals. Especially' – he paused for a moment and looked around – 'in this setting. They offend my aesthetic sense.'

Dupré gave a quick, dry laugh. 'So you like Alpiniano's cave, Dr. Merten?'

'Yes. As you told me that you kept your treasures elsewhere, I had of course no idea that elsewhere was so near.' Again, Dupré laughed, this time quite good-naturedly. 'Who was Alpiniano?' Merten ventured.

There was a pause. Had Dupré not heard the question? He had – and when he spoke, his voice sounded strained.

'None of the people here, at Opaco, know. I had tried to find out for years. And as I lived at Alpiniano's Court, I eventually decided to turn this into Alpiniano's cave. This' – with a sweeping gesture he indicated the statues, furniture and pictures around them – 'is the work of a lifetime. My life.' Dupré held up one of his sleeves. 'Have you seen my clothes, Dr. Merten?' As he leant forward and pointed to the precious embroidery on his shirt, he almost shouted. 'Down here, I am Alpiniano! This is my realm! And you, more than anyone ever, have become a threat to my existence!' He seemed near to losing his self-control and was obviously struggling with himself. There was even a sound like a sob. For the first time, Merten wondered whether the man was mad.

When Dupré spoke again, he was absolutely calm. 'I appreciate your intelligence, Dr. Merten – I have in fact learnt a few things from you. I therefore wish to enlighten you as well. In other words: I wish to be completely frank with you about my plans for today. As our friend Walter Cesini languishes in custody, I have to prevent you from revealing things you know to his host the district attorney. And you know, or guess, far too much. I may as well tell you that I do have your diary.'

Dupré paused and Merten thought how lucky it was that he had not mentioned the attorney in his notes.

'Unfortunately,' Dupré continued, 'Gastone featured quite prominently in your writing. And he collected you at the airport after you had written your last entry! I was never sure how much he knew about me – but given your presence here and your inquisitive mind, he was dangerous. As I said, unfortunately. May I say, Dr. Merten, that I regret it even more that you are going to have an accident.'

Merten knew that he had to play for time – it was still a good hour before Davide would ring Talon. And then, the attorney's men would still have to get to Dupré's place!

'May I know what kind of an accident I am going to have?' he inquired.

'Turn down the music!' Dupré said to the marshal.

'Can you hear those dogs?' Dupré asked after it had become quiet in the crypt? Merten looked at him without replying. 'Well, this dear friend of ours – my step-brother in, fact' – Dupré pointed to the sacristan – 'is going to give you an injection. You will be heavily sedated. The coachman will then drive you out into the woods. May I leave the rest to your imagination? As a resident here, you have probably heard that our dogs are reputed to be rather savage.'

He had, Merten said – 'and,' he added, pointing to the sacristan, 'I'd love to take this goddamned old crook out there with me!' He realized his best chance was to keep Dupré talking.

It seemed Dupré did not need to be prompted. 'If only you had never set eyes on that fresco in the café, Dr. Merten,' he said whiningly – 'if you hadn't, you and I could enjoy an idyllic relationship.'

Merten admitted the idea had not occurred to him. 'You would have to change your friends, though,' he said, indicating the marshal, the coachman and the sacristan.

Dupré seemed not to have heard him. 'Cesini,' he continued, 'was terrified when years ago you started frequenting the café. He thought that you knew the original picture and would at some stage realize that it had been substituted by a copy.'

'I didn't at the time.'

'Well, he thought you might. Hence, he decided to turn his copy into a rather different picture.'

Merten laughed. 'Master Cesini's misfortune was that I noticed the metamorphosis of the courtesan. In fact, that's what triggered me off: I saw how the lady in the portrait changed gradually. Cesini's copy of Samira was good. After his changes, the picture was rubbish.' Although Dupré knew it was him who had a few days previously spotted the courtesan's dripping hair, Merten was careful not to mention the concoction he suspected Cesini to have used – he knew that otherwise Dupré would probably guess that he was in touch with the district attorney. He asked Dupré why Cesini had made the courtesan resemble his ex-wife.

Dupré's answer tied in with Amaranta's explanation, and was delivered rather relishingly. 'He just felt that he catered to some – shall we say – lusts of yours.'

'So what about the weeping statue?' Merten asked.

Dupré frowned. 'To tell you honestly, Dr. Merten, I was never happy about this madonna business. Originally, it was just a whim of Cesini's, who at the time was into a variety of experiments with paint and gels.' Again, Merten remembered the lesson given to him by the innkeeper at Brionnac. 'But after he had had to apply his own blood to the cheeks of the madonna – the person creating trouble was of course that district attorney – there was no stopping him. Nor my step-bother here,' Dupré said, pointing to the sacristan. 'Had that idiotic mayor not performed a u-turn, the whole thing would probably have died down. Also, we did of course not reckon with the media – nor with your return to Fluentia, Dr. Merten! Anyway, I dare say Cesini eventually excelled in making the madonna weep. The man knows about everything, be it paint, be it chemicals. He should be a teacher. Or, like you, a scholar.'

'Or a cook,' Merten said.

'I beg your pardon?'

Merten laughed and said he was only joking.

Dupré seemed nonplussed for a moment. 'Anyway,' he resumed, 'once Cesini had set up his stall, the whole thing started making him money. Imagine: it was the first time in the man's life that he had a steady income. He is, by the way, a rather good sculptor. Don't judge him by his replicas of the madonna – these were for the indiscriminating masses.'

Dupré's recitation confirmed what his visitor had been suspecting; but whilst the man talked, something else had attracted Merten's attention. Dupré noticed, and his eye followed Merten's.

'Ah,' he said, 'I was waiting for this! What does your infallible eye tell you, Dr. Merten?'

This time, it was Merten, staring at a wingless Cupid, who looked nonplussed. 'It's the statue which was offered in the Sirconi sale,' he exclaimed – 'the God of Love!'

Dupré clapped his hands. 'Bravo!'

'So you are the person who bought it after the auction?'

'I am indeed,' Dupré said with a theatrical bow. 'Which means,' he added, 'that I bought it more cheaply – but it still cost me a lot of money.'

'Congratulations,' Merten said dryly; 'but tell me: why were you convinced that my attribution was correct?'

Dupré smiled. 'When I was still a boy, my father gave me an old book with letters by the powerful men in Fluentia's heyday. I devoured these letters – I probably still know some of them by heart. When I read your catalogue entry I remembered that I too had read of the "figure" for the Grand Duke's fountain. I checked in my book. Unlike the letter you quoted from, which was by the artist, mine was by the Grand Duke – and it was far more detailed. And' – Dupré paused – 'I have news for you. That figure' – Dupré pointed to the statue – 'did not embellish the fountain! Contrary to what I said to you when we met at Berenice's, you did not get *all* the details right. That figure – *my* figure – was the modello. The Grand Duke gives the exact measurements for both modello and the two figures on the fountain. The latter were bigger. But anyway, you were correct about the artist. Once more: my compliments, Dr. Merten. Isn't it strange how, in a way, our relationship began long before we met ...'

Merten laughed. 'Given what you must have paid for the figure, the relationship cost you dearly!'

Dupré raised his hands appeasingly. 'Actually, I can absolve you on that account. You might say that' – Dupré stopped, and then continued with a grand gesture – 'that I got the statue for free.'

'How come?'

'Well,' Dupré continued slowly, 'it has to do with what I just said about Cesini: that he is a rather good sculptor.'

'So?'

'So I asked him to make a replica – which I then sold abroad as the original. And for a better price than the real thing here.'

What a crook! What crooks! Merten, looking at the four rogues surrounding him, had to make an effort to keep calm.

'You see, Dr. Merten, whereas I had to use Cesini's copy of the courtesan fresco to cover his theft of the original, I acquired this statue lawfully. You will admit that parting with any work of art is painful – which was why, in this case, I decided to let go of the replica.'

Merten could not help laughing at the man's hypocrisy. 'Who has the replica now?' he wanted to know. Dupré shook his head. 'This I am not telling you. And anyway, Dr. Merten: question time is up.'

Merten, who had managed to consult his watch again, realized that things looked bad. It was still over half an hour before Davide would ring Talon – and, it suddenly occurred to him, the attorney might be at lunch. He looked at the four of them. The coachman worried him most – Merten, although no longer feeling handicapped by his past operation, knew that he could not match the man's raw strength. With this one he would have to rely on his wits. If only, before facing the coachman, he could eliminate two of the others

– but to have a chance without his gun, he needed to get closer to them.

'Would you,' he asked Dupré, 'at least allow me to have another close look at the statue? It's years since I last examined it.'

Dupré was clearly fascinated. 'You have no idea, Dr. Merten, how much I admire your request. You are a dedicated scholar to the very last. Please!' He pointed invitingly in the direction of the wingless Cupid. Merten walked over to the statue and lifted it up very carefully.

'How I would have loved to work with you!' Dupré continued. Again, Merten thought he heard a sob.

He moved into the light and turned the figure in his hands. The marshal stood nearest to him, and in spite of his adverse circumstances he found the inspiration that in a moment this man would be the first one to receive his attentions strangely elevating.

'The statue was actually brought here for your benefit. I normally keep it in a small adjoining chamber,' Dupré declared. 'In fact' – he snapped his fingers – 'the coachman will take it there again right now.'

Merten, who concluded this was good news for him, put the statue down and stepped back as if to look at it from a different angle. In doing so, he had moved within less than three feet of the marshal. As the coachman picked up his charge, Dupré yelled at him to take care. The man was obviously more skilled in handling bodies than art works, Merten thought. They all watched him as he disappeared through a small door with the statue.

When, out of nowhere, Merten's fist landed on the marshal's chin, the sound of bones splintering was ugly. The man folded up instantly, without even knowing what had happened to him.

The sacristan dashed forward; Merten realized that like him, the man was after his gun, which the marshal had pocketed. He had underestimated the old fellow's agility; the sacristan already had his hands in one of the marshal's pockets when he caught him by the throat and pulled him up. It had been the wrong pocket. He hurled the sacristan against one of the stone pillars, bent down and shifted the marshal who seemed to be lying on the pocket with the gun. There was a shot, and Merten felt a sharp pain. He looked across to the pulpit, from where the shot had come. Dupré held a small revolver in his hand. It was still pointed at Merten.

The pain was intense. The coachman, who came running back like a mad bull, seized him by the shoulders, and Merten screamed. He could see that his shirt underneath the left shoulder was turning red.

'Why did you have to do this, Dr. Merten? Once more, you are throwing me into complete disarray!' Dupré waved the coachman aside and told the sacristan, who steadied himself against the pillar, to look at Merten's arm and stop the bleeding. Limping badly, the sacristan came over.

'With a bullet inside you, we have to forget about the dogs,' Dupré announced – 'it wouldn't look like an accident.'

Again, Merten screamed; the sacristan, who attended to him, was rather rough. But when he looked at his arm, the bleeding seemed to have stopped. Meanwhile, Dupré had stepped down from the pulpit and started talking *sotto voce* to the coachman. Finally, he came over to Merten, who now sat in a chair and held on to his arm.

'I am afraid, Dr. Merten, I shall have to dispose of you in a more orthodox fashion. We have to get rid of your body. Your dead body, I mean. The coachman here, whom you have not managed to endear yourself to, says he wants to break your neck. But more importantly: we do have some friends up in the hills who have a special interest in human remains.'

Merten, feeling weak, shuddered. First, he thought of Gastone's end and of the coroner's suspicions about the steward's neck – and then he remembered Gastone's remarks about dead bodies being boiled in cauldrons. Although he had dismissed both Gastone's and Pepalmar's hints as to a Satanist coven, he realised now that in the hills above Opaco there obviously were people dabbling in the occult.

So this is it, he thought – there seemed to be no way out. He looked around the crypt. All at once, he was intrigued again by the picture on the wall behind the pulpit. Just like in the case of the wingless Cupid, Dupré's eye followed his.

'A copy, needless to say. But,' Dupré added, 'you undoubtedly know the original.' Merten just nodded. 'You see, Dr. Merten: at one stage, having realised how much of a threat you were to me and all that I am, I felt like the protagonist in this picture – I thought I would commit suicide and at the same time destroy all the things I had loved. Everything you see around you! But then I changed my mind. After all' – suddenly, Dupré's voice sounded shrill again – 'I am Alpiniano!' He turned to the coachman. 'I want you to go upstairs and close the door from the lounge to the crypt! Afterwards' – he pointed at Merten – 'this man is yours.'

At this moment, the marshal groaned and the coachman knelt down by his side.

Dupré, however, looked at the picture again. 'You could argue that the female slave in the foreground looks a bit like your housekeeper.' Merten did not reply, but had to admit to himself that Dupré had a point. Was it the woman's voluptuousness which struck a chord? Even with a dagger raised to her throat, she seemed to vibrate as she would have done whilst being caressed.

Since the marshal, despite his friend's efforts to revive him, did not move, the coachman got up and walked through the door with the spiral staircase.

'I hasten to add that the likeness is not a deliberate attempt of Cesini's,' Dupré went on. 'But may I nevertheless invite you to imagine the naked slave girl as your beloved Amaranta, and the man behind her as our excellent coachman.'

'You are mad!' Merten exclaimed. The whole picture was a holocaust of orgasm and death.

Dupré shook his head reprovingly. 'Amaranta knows too much, Dr. Merten – your diary leaves no doubt. This is what's going to happen to her.' Dupré studied the picture with the detached interest of an anatomist. 'The coachman will cut her throat. He will probably want to enjoy her carnally before – just look at the way she writhes and arches her back!' Dupré was suddenly seized with a fit of high-pitched laughter. 'As I said to you a little while ago, Dr. Merten: I wish to be completely frank with you. I wish to enlighten you before you embark on your final journey.'

Merten was in no mood to comment – but he now knew for certain that the man was a dangerous lunatic. He had to get out of here! Whilst they looked at each other, there was a thudding noise from somewhere above them. And then another.

When the coachman appeared again, he no longer stood on his feet. His body came down the stairs by jerks, head first. As the body lacked motive power, a succession of energetic kicks courtesy of some still unseen agent facilitated its transfer from stairs to crypt. Once the coachman had cleared the stairs and joined his brother in arms the supine marshal, Davide came bounding through the door – and from this moment, things happened in quick succession. The revolver was back in Dupré's hand. Before Dupré could take aim at the lad, Merten jumped from his seat and crashed his good arm against the man's wrist. The shot went into the vaulted ceiling and the revolver sailed across the floor to the far end of the crypt. Merten fell back into his chair – the pain in his left shoulder was maddening. The rest was like in a film. He saw Davide take care of Dupré – and he shouted as he noticed how the sacristan was stealing away towards the door with the spiral staircase. But all at once, the crypt was alive with poker-faced men in grey suits. Before everything went black, Merten saw the sacristan being handcuffed.

10

A Nymph Turns Into Water

This morning, one of Constantin Talon's men brought over the diary. It is the day after my almost fatal adventure, and they are still searching Dupré's house. The attorney's concern for me is most touching; in fact, everybody's is. Yesterday, Talon did not even leave until the local doctor had come and dressed my arm. Apparently, the bullet has gone right through, which to me sounds good news. It was also Talon who told me that I owe my escape to Davide and Amaranta. What had dawned upon me late had occurred to them straightaway: that, had they waited a whole hour and a half for me to come back, the attorney would almost certainly have been at lunch. Therefore, Amaranta rang him an hour after I had left and Davide ventured over to Alpiniano's Court before the detectives turned up. Davide must have arrived upstairs shortly after I was shot at, because he overheard Dupré announcing his new arrangements for my disposal. Just as Dupré had played into my hands before, his sending the coachman upstairs of course suited Davide. He has assured me that he was most grateful for the opportunity – he says the coachman had once or twice treated him very badly when he was a child. And also that when he heard what the man was going to do to his mother, he just hit the roof.

As I want to forget yesterday – for a while at least – I started rereading the diary as soon as I got it back. But then, unexpectedly, Silvana and my daughter stood on my doorstep. Pepalmar, who had telephoned me last night, had afterwards also called them. I was delighted to see little Sylvie, but I must have been a disappointment to her; even in the morning, I felt very tired. The child sounds so precocious – is it possible that she guesses something about me and her? I must speak to Silvana in private. But apart from her very own worries she now has new ones. Apparently, her mother is ailing, and she says she may have to fly back to her country, as looking after her young son could be too much for the old lady.

After Silvana's and Sylvie's visit, I reread my diary from beginning to end. And as I am in need of distraction, I decided I might as well add a new entry. The truth is: my arm still hurts, and it also feels swollen. But surely this is just part of the healing process. Anyway, I do not want to tell Amaranta. She already does more than enough for me, and I have a feeling she did not close an eye last night, which she spent here in the villa. Her sensitivity still surprises me – very likely, my early obsession with her, or rather with one particular feature of hers, has not been the best preparation I could have given myself for a caring relationship! It is obvious that Gastone's death and now my experience have shaken her very badly.

What else? My thoughts keep returning to my early entries. When reading the diary again, I found it strange that in the Fluentia sections I never talked in detail about the temple of St. John the Baptist. Strange, because I had promised to do so, and also because I studied this unique edifice both outside and inside on many occasions. Needless to say that I went there more than once since my return this spring. I have always been intrigued by the Baptist's story – hence it was probably inevitable that on each visit to the temple his portrayals by different artists claimed my attention. He is even present on and above the doors. And so is Salome! It still strikes me as odd that a man in whose goodwill and powers so many maidens, their mothers and also widows have believed throughout the ages owed his terrible end to a woman. However difficult a time the Baptist had in Judaea, he should have stayed there; when he left to preach east of the Jordan, he walked out of the frying-pan into the fire. Anyway,

I am glad that in the depictions I am referring to, his gruesome end is not dwelt upon. And that the sculptor responsible for the south door of the temple portrayed the final scene between Salome and her mother in a low key as well – unlike that painter who, in a picture I saw in another country, presents the girl as an eye-catcher and makes her hold the platter with the head of the Baptist aloft in the way an athlete exhibits a trophy! But my mind is going astray. I want to talk to Amaranta. Dinner will be ready soon – and I shall insist that my guardian angel goes back to her place for the night. She needs to unwind.

★ ★ ★ ★ ★

Amaranta had a good night's sleep, whereas I was restless. As I sometimes do when I can't get something out of my mind, I even dreamed about St. John the Baptist. What worries me, however, is that my arm is very swollen and red. Although I have kept quiet about this, I admitted to Amaranta when we had lunch that I feel a bit dizzy. I had to – given that she cooked a wonderful meal and that I then ate very little. She insisted that I should go upstairs and sleep all afternoon. But unlike her, the child of nature, I can only rarely sleep during the day. Hence, once more, I am pouring myself into my diary. The Baptist's story still goes round and round in my head. How did he, a man with wild imaginings and at the same time a special message, manage to live on locusts and honey? And how did Salome end? One story has it that she fell into a freezing river and that her head, trapped between pieces of ice, was severed from her body. There is of course no truth in this; and yet, as I write it down I sit here – on a hot day – and am shivering.

Why can't I ban all these images from my mind? Especially Salome's lascivious dancing, which cost the Baptist his head! Perhaps I should go for a walk – or at least sit by the open window and take in the sights and sounds which captivated me so utterly when I first arrived here. But I can't even get up. And now – I have just heard a bell from the village up on the hillside – I see somebody dancing again. But it is not Herod's birthday, it is St. John's Eve. And the dancer, in front of a bonfire, is Amaranta. Why, then, do I see her with a platter in her hands? Does it matter? There is little doubt that I too, as a result of a woman's dancing, lost my head. Again, I cannot get up. I am very unwell – even writing is painful. In fact, I feel as if I were drowning ... which I have always imagined as the most terrible way to die. If only we could walk on water: how wonderful that would be! Just like, after the death of the Baptist, the man from Nazareth. Having at first withdrawn to a remote place, he went out to join the disciples, whose boat was already a considerable distance from land. And when they beheld him, they saw him walk on the lake, and ...

★ ★ ★ ★ ★

It was weeks after the incident at Alpiniano's Court, and he sat in the garden of the villa. He had fallen asleep while trying to put his more recent experiences into chronological order. When he woke up, his attention was monopolized by Amaranta who, not far but turned away from him, leaned on the stone parapet and looked out into the surrounding hills. What a sight she was!

'Strange Fruit,' he said.

'What?' She had turned around instantly.

'Strange Fruit,' he repeated, still somewhat dopey.

The moment he saw her worried look, he was wide awake. 'It's the nickname I had given you when lusting after your bottom, years ago in the Fluentia café.'

With a merry laugh, she first kissed him and then lowered herself to sit astride him on his deckchair. 'If my bottom is on your thoughts, you must be well again, dearest Leander.' She looked at him, and her bronzed face with its arched eyebrows struck him as magic. 'Tell me then: do you still like me a little?'

He did not understand what she was getting at and said so.

Again, she laughed. 'You confused me with Salome in your diary – I must say, I was not flattered!' What did she, he wondered, know about his diary? She guessed his thought. 'I told you how I found out when you were in hospital, but it was probably not the right time.'

He told her that he still did not remember everything, and she kissed him again.

'When I found you unconscious on the floor of the study, your diary lay open on the desk, with your pen across it. I felt for your pulse, which was fast, and then curiosity prompted me to glance at what you had last written. It made me do the right thing: I telephoned the ambulance. I remembered how, when I was a girl, a man came into my father's bar stone-cold sober and started hallucinating. Although my father suggested the hospital, the police drove the man back to his home. A few days later he was dead; he had had – like you – blood poisoning.'

She got up after a while, saying she had to do a few things in the house. As he was alone, his thoughts returned to what he had started contemplating while, when lucid again, still in hospital: that he would resign from his museum job in his native country. He did not want to live there any longer – and although it was his ancestral home, he was ready to sell the stately pile at Charlottenfels. Pepalmar had told him on more than one occasion that, with his qualifications, he would have no difficulty finding a good job in Fluentia or in the neighbouring provinces, where some big towns boasted great art collections; but the professor had also said that it might be just as good an idea not to seek employment and instead use his research notes to concentrate on writing books. Whether or not, at Opaco, he would continue to live in the villa remained to be seen – but he already knew that he would not let go of his mother's house at Brionnac. Although he had not mentioned any of this to Amaranta, he felt that she would not be averse to adopting Brionnac as a second home; she had been quite excited when one day, after his return from there, he had suggested that perhaps she would like to visit the place with him. And of course she also spoke the language of the people there. Davide would not be a problem. Merten had decided that, whatever his and Amaranta's circumstances, he was going to pay for the lad to attend the agricultural college. Davide himself had mentioned the place twice when he visited Merten in hospital – apparently Gastone, who had been a student at the college when a young man, had told him interesting things about it.

The thought of Gastone made Merten get up and walk over to the parapet. On one of his last days in hospital, Constantin Talon had telephoned Amaranta: the coachman, the district attorney said, had admitted to murdering the steward. As he looked across the landscape before him, Amaranta came walking down the steps and through the garden.

She held out a letter to him. 'This arrived in the morning. But as you kept falling asleep soon after breakfast, I decided I wouldn't give it to you straight away. No doubt the stamp and the handwriting will tell you who the sender is.' She paused. 'You were still feverish when she left. But she promised that she would write to you soon – which is why I kept quiet both about her and your little daughter.'

The letter was a long one. Amaranta had gone to the co-operative to buy some wine, and he knew that she just wanted him to be on his own while reading. So Silvana was back in her country! In the letter she said she did not know how long for – but maybe for ever. A lot depended on the children; and she could definitely no longer rely on her mother to look after them. She had left Fluentia when he was still in a poor state, but she said she knew then through Amaranta that the doctors had started him on the antibiotics and that he was out of danger. He smiled when she vented her anger on 'that villainous sacristan,' having no doubt poisoned his wound – in fact, the doctors in the hospital had told him as soon as he was fully conscious that it was the bullet itself which had caused the complications. He was touched when she referred to how Amaranta had cared for him, bringing all his cassettes into hospital and playing his favourite music. Looking up and breathing in the scents from the surrounding trees and garden, he concluded that Amaranta had been right – the soul, she had insisted, needed its medicines as well.

When he continued reading, it was with the feeling that a surprise was still to come. He was not mistaken. 'Sylvie,' the girl's mother wrote, 'cannot understand why you didn't tell her that you are her father. When she first mentioned it, I was stunned. I wanted to know what made her say such a thing. She said she had known the moment you started talking to her outside the café – that nobody had ever talked to her like that. And then again at Opaco. She also says that whenever, while she was still smaller, I had mentioned you to her, she realized that you were special. So there you are: if you want to write to her, as I am sure you will, the door is wide open.' For a moment, he closed his eyes – but then he read on. 'When all of a sudden I had to leave, Amaranta kindly suggested that for the time being Sylvie could stay at the villa and that she would look after her – but as she hardly knows me and the child, I felt I could not impose on her. Which, dear Leander, prompts another thought. It seems, as you once more need to recuperate, that you are destined not to go back to Charlottenfels. Whatever you decide – and please, Leander, forgive me for being so blunt: if you let go of the present lady in your life, you are a fool.'

★ ★ ★ ★ ★

He had continued living in the villa. Once again, it was getting hot – summer had begun, and the trial of Dupré and his accomplices was imminent. Merten knew from Constantin Talon that the main defendant had dismissed his counsel and was going to conduct his case single-handedly. Apparently, Dupré intended to whitewash himself by pushing logic to its very limits. Thus, he had argued all through pre-trial detention that as long as the Samira fresco in the café gave pleasure to whoever looked at it, the fact that it was a copy by Cesini did not matter; and he had craftily supported his claim by pointing out that the north door of the temple of Saint John the Baptist, admired by hundreds of thousands, was a also copy – a replica financed, when the original was in need of restoration and afterwards of a location where it would not deteriorate again, by some foreign group! The district attorney admitted that he relished the challenge; the trial, he said, would not only go down in the chronicles of Fluentia, it might even make respectable art collectors – if not experts – question their own ethics.

Meanwhile, at Opaco, the statue was back in the garden of the villager who had originally acquired it as a souvenir. And not only were people who wanted to see it now charged a fee: the owner did rather well, as there were innumerable visitors who still believed in a miracle. Tears, however, there were none; the madonna had dried up. With Cesini in jail, there was nobody to attend to her – be it by sprinkling her cheeks with his own blood, as Cesini had done on one occasion, be it by applying concoctions to her eyebrows that liquefied in high temperatures or when the statue was moved. Merten knew from Constantin Talon that, in custody, Cesini had been quite co-operative. Unlike Dupré and the sacristan. The latter, the district attorney said, was one of the biggest liars he had ever come across.

As Merten expected a visitor, the forthcoming trial did not much occupy his mind. And on a Thursday, he got the call he had been waiting for. Her departure time had just been announced, the distant voice said – she was leaving in less than two hours. Was he happy to see her again, she then asked tentatively.

'Very happy,' he answered – 'just a little bit nervous.' She seemed to find his admission rather funny.

At the airport, the morning after, he had little time to consider his emotional state. Moments after he had walked into the arrivals hall he spotted her – obviously, her plane had landed early. Those eyes, he thought; and he remembered the day when, at Pepalmar's, the coin had dropped as he stood opposite her mother. But the child had seen him as well. She came running up to him and hugged him. All of a sudden, he felt like a child himself. He was grateful to Amaranta for insisting that he went to the airport on his own; as usual when it came to matters of the heart, she saw things more clearly than he.

★ ★ ★ ★ ★

Two days after Sylvie's arrival, Merten had taken the girl up to the village to see the madonna. It had been at her request. From there, they had driven to Fonteluce. Merten knew that she loved the sweets and ice cream produced in and around Fluentia, and apart from going to treat her to what she had no doubt missed, he also wanted her to see the spectacular view, from the very top of Fonteluce, onto Fluentia and its great cathedral. When they sat at a table outside the hotel in the square, Sylvie again started talking about the events in connection with the madonna – back at home, her mother Silvana had told her what she knew, and after her arrival at the villa Amaranta had entertained her with some of the more colourful episodes.

'Babbo,' the child asked, 'did you ever hit that coachman?' She had already told him in the car from the airport to Opaco that, to distinguish between him and Silvana's ex-husband, whom she had always called Papa, she would call him Babbo.

Merten laughed. 'No,' he said, 'and I am glad I didn't try!'

He told her that unfortunately the young man who did hit the coachman was not around – but that if one day she decided to visit for more than just a couple of weeks, she would certainly meet him.

When they left Fonteluce, he chose a very scenic road. And on their drive down towards the suburbs of Fluentia, he told her the names of the neighbouring hills and of the great villas and the two or three castles they passed.

'Mama told me,' Sylvie said, 'how she loved your stories when the two of you started meeting in Fluentia.' He smiled wistfully. The child was silent for a while, and the road with its bends claimed his full attention. They were approaching a little bridge when she spoke again. 'Tell me, Babbo,' she said, 'do you know a love story?'

He did not have to think long. 'Yes,' he said, pointing to the little bridge – 'and it has to be told right there.' He stopped the car.

'Why there?' Sylvie wanted to know.

'You will find out,' he said, putting his hand on hers – 'let's go and sit on the bridge.'

It was a simple stone bridge, and when they sat on one of its low walls, he looked down into the water for inspiration. In summer, the river was barely more than a trickle.

'Dearest Sylvie,' he finally said, 'this is a story – a poem, actually – by one of the greatest storytellers of all times; but I am not sure if I remember it very well.'

The child gave him the same disarming smile she had given him when they met for the first time, outside the café in Fluentia. 'But it's you, Babbo, who is telling it – that's all that matters!'

He loved her enthusiasm; it made him rise to the occasion.

'This is a very ancient landscape,' he said, taking in the hills and the woods above them with a sweeping gesture. 'Up there, at a well near Fonteluce, the goddess Diana and her companions used to gather at sunset, singing sweet melodies. Sometimes, the nymphs would bathe in the clear water. But the goddess warned them: by no means, if ever a man approached them, should they listen to him. Whoever did not heed her words, she – Diana – would punish her most severely.'

The child looked perplexed. 'But, Babbo, weren't you going to tell me a love story?'

He smiled. 'I am just about to begin, darling.'

He told her how one day, a young shepherd became the accidental witness of the meeting between Diana and her nymphs. How the youth fell in love with one of the nymphs – whom he did not dare approach, because he feared Diana's bow and arrows. He did manage to catch the name of the nymph, though, before the whole company vanished; and when Venus and her son visited him in a dream, he implored them to help him find his beloved.

'And did he?' Sylvie interrupted.

'Yes – but the nymph, mindful of Diana's warning, fled. Eventually, the lovesick shepherd became so desperate that he felt only a sacrifice would grant him a hearing from Venus. And indeed: after he had slaughtered one of his lambs, Venus and her son appeared to him again. She had been moved by his gesture and invocation, Venus said, and would henceforth guide him.'

Again, Sylvie tried to interrupt, but Merten would not let her. He told her that, shortly after, it occurred to the shepherd that his mother had a beautiful dress which she hardly ever wore. And how the youth took that dress, put it on and in it instantly looked like a nymph himself. And that in this guise, he one day chanced upon the nymphs again, who befriended him and invited him to join them naked in the well. 'The shepherd was careful to be the last one to take off his clothes. Once in the water, he held on to his beloved, swearing everlasting faithfulness to her. And while all the other nymphs fled, he made his sweetheart believe in his vows.'

'Is this the end of the story?'

He got up. 'No,' he said – 'although I wish the famous and eloquent poet would grant a pardon here, and let the tale move on soberly.' He walked the few steps to the end of the bridge, and from there a few more steps down to the water. The child, from above, kept watching him.

'After the nymph had yielded to the shepherd's lovemaking,' he continued, 'they parted. They had agreed where they would next meet again. But when the day came, the shepherd waited in vain – the nymph had regretted her disobedience to the goddess Diana. The youth, who felt rejected, was finally overcome by despair. He walked down to a small river and, having called out the name of the nymph one last time, put his own dagger through his heart. Ever since then the river, once red with the shepherd's blood, has born that young man's name.'

'Is this the river?' Sylvie gasped, pointing down from the bridge.

Her father smiled. 'No. It's somewhere over there.' He looked in the direction where the sun was slowly setting.

'Shall we go there?' she asked.

He shook his head. He said she was fine where she was – and he then told her that early in the year after the shepherd's death, the nymph gave birth to a little boy. And that one day, while out in the hills with the little boy, the nymph spotted Diana and her retinue. 'Terrified, she hid her child and ran away. But Diana saw her, and at the same time the child started crying. When the goddess saw the nymph approach a river, she called out. *Oh, silly sinner! Do not attempt to escape – for against my wish, you will never cross the water*! Once more, the nymph did not heed Diana's words. And when she set foot in the water, Diana raised her hand, demanding that the river retain the fugitive. And in a moment's space, the unlucky nymph turned into water.'

Merten paused. 'This, by the way, is the river. It – and the bridge on which you are sitting – is named after the nymph.'

He waited for his daughter to say something. When, a moment later, he joined her on the bridge again, he saw that she was crying.

'They were just not meant to be together, the nymph and her shepherd,' she said between sobs. He sat down and put his arm around her. 'Don't forget that this is a tale by a great storyteller,' he finally said. Sylvie looked at him questioningly.

'The two lovers have long been united – in fact, ever since Diana's intervention.' From the bridge, he pointed down the river. 'Somewhere down there, the two rivers, this one and the one which bears the shepherd's name, merge and continue as one stream.'

The child, who had stood up, looked intently into the distance.

'So, how did you like the story, Sylvie?'

When she turned round, her radiant smile once again reminded him of their first meeting. 'It is a wonderful story, Babbo – thank you!' she said, embracing him at the same time.

He too had got up again. 'I must tell you something else,' he said, as they walked away from the bridge and towards the car. She waited for what was to come – and as they sat in the car, he turned the mirror above the dashboard towards her. 'Look at your eyes, Sylvie,' he said as he started the engine. She did as she was told, but wanted to know why. 'Well, it's just that the writer whose story I told you also invented you and your mother. Long before both of you were born.' The child looked puzzled. 'This writer,' her father continued, 'wanted the eyes of his ideal woman to be almond-shaped; with a vivid' – he smiled – 'sometimes even slightly roguish expression in them.' Merten paused. And then he added that the great writer was obviously describing her, Sylvie's, and Silvana's eyes. The child was fascinated and bent forward to study her face. As he drove off, he felt obliged to offer an apology for turning the mirror back.

By the time they reached the road to Opaco, Sylvie looked somehow downcast.

'But, Babbo,' she finally said, 'Amaranta doesn't have almond-shaped eyes!' Rather amused, he admitted that she was right. 'What I mean,' she said feelingly: 'Isn't it quite sad, for both of you?' The villa had come in sight, and Merten laughed.

'Darling, not everyone can have the same eyes. But have you noticed Amaranta's eyebrows?' He did not wait for an answer. 'Such eyebrows, arched and strong in the centre, were considered one of the foremost assets of a beauty by another distinguished poet in ancient Fluentia. Hence' – he gave his daughter a tender smile as they stopped in front of the wine making co-operative – 'Amaranta is not really that much at a disadvantage.'

Sylvie said she was very glad. 'So did that other poet,' she wanted to know, 'invent Amaranta?'

They had walked through the garden to the back of the villa, and as they approached the steps, Amaranta appeared on top. What a woman, he once more thought – remembering at that very moment his early adolescence at Charlottenfels and how, in solitary hours, the thought of a woman with similar physical attributes had caused him endless bewilderment.

'Did you hear me, Babbo?' the girl persisted.

He answered in the affirmative – and then he said that perhaps, long before he read the said Fluentia poets, a boy called Leander Frédéric Merten had invented Amaranta as he lay awake at night.